There had to be a way out of this.

Even with her military training, a fight against someone who knew her and her background would be a lot more difficult than an altercation with a neighborhood punk. There was no way to know how many intruders were in the building or how heavily armed they were. No intel meant an unfair fight.

The beeping of the alarm gained speed. All she had to do was hang tight and stay hidden for another five minutes. The police tended to arrive quickly once the alarm notified them. After last year's break-in and vandalism, they didn't play when it came to this school.

"We should have waited till it was dark." The twanging on the edges of the voice was somehow familiar. Somehow, somewhere she'd heard that voice before. Meghan dug for a memory, for a face, but came up empty save the bizarre feeling she shouldn't be afraid.

Jodie Bailey writes novels about freedom and the heroes who fight for it. Her novel *Crossfire* won a 2015 RT Reviewers' Choice Best Love Inspired Suspense Book Award. She is convinced a camping trip to the beach with her family, a good cup of coffee and a great book can cure all ills. Jodie lives in North Carolina with her husband, her daughter and two dogs.

Books by Jodie Bailey

Love Inspired Suspense

Freefall
Crossfire
Smokescreen
Compromised Identity
Breach of Trust

BREACH OF TRUST

JODIE BAILEY

HARLEQUIN® LOVE INSPIRED® SUSPENSE

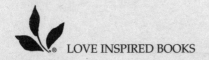

LOVE INSPIRED BOOKS

Recycling programs
for this product may
not exist in your area.

ISBN-13: 978-0-373-44768-8

Breach of Trust

Copyright © 2016 by Jodie Bailey

www.Harlequin.com

Printed in U.S.A.

Forget the former things; do not dwell on the past.
See, I am doing a new thing! Now it springs up;
do you not perceive it? I am making a way in the wilderness
and streams in the wasteland.
—Isaiah 43:18-19

To my cousin Ben.

Who else?

Without your manual push mower, Tate—and this book—never would have existed.

Here it is forever in print: you were a trendsetter with penguin firefighters before they were cool.

ONE

Meghan McGuire dragged her fingers through her short dark hair and scanned the computer screen, fighting an uncharacteristic cold sweat at the message swimming in blue on the display.

It's time for round two.

He'd returned. The short series of numbers he used as a signature followed the message, leaving no room for doubt. More than a decade of silence, enough time to stop looking over her shoulder…and still he'd returned. Here. On her last day as technology director at a tiny private school on the outskirts of Flint, Michigan.

If she'd left yesterday, her official last day… If she'd denied principal Yvonne Craft's request to run through the system one more time… If she'd left at seven, the way she'd planned… Any of those things, and she'd be at the farmhouse, painting window casings with Phoebe instead of sitting here, her life crumbling right as she was about to step into her dreams coming true. Right as she was about to start a whole new season.

At thirty-one, she'd had plenty of those already. But

when it came to this one? Aside from the day she'd joined the army, this had been the first she'd really been excited about. Working with her friend Phoebe Snyder's charitable foundation, Meghan was putting the finishing touches on a foster home for the most desperate of lost children.

And she wasn't going to let the past steal it. Not without a fight. Rolling her neck to the side to stretch out the tension, she reached for her backpack and an external drive. She could download an image of the system and—

A sudden series of thuds bounced along the hallway and the alarm panel by the front door started its incessant beeping, demanding someone feed it the correct code before it called the police.

"We've got about two minutes before the cops start this way." The voice, coarse and unfamiliar, scraped into the office and grated against Meghan's ears.

Her fingers tightened around the straps of the backpack. No one she knew was supposed to be in the building this late.

And no one she knew would worry about the police, either.

Meghan slipped to the closed office door and pressed her back tight against the wall to listen, recalling long-unused training to keep her breathing even. The church housing the school wasn't in the best of neighborhoods, and they'd suffered one other break-in, when vandals nearly destroyed the school. Her car parked under the awning by the front door should have been a clue to any aspiring burglar trying for an easy score that the building was occupied.

But maybe that was the point. If they were hoping

to find someone in the building…well, that was more than she wanted to think about. And she'd be sure to give them a fight they never anticipated.

It had been a long time since she'd been involved in a physical altercation, but she'd been trained well. Meghan stiffened her stance, charged by the prospect of action. Anybody who broke into this building had no idea what they were in for.

"Her car's out front. She's here. Find her." The rough masculine voice echoed from the hallway. "Get her into the van. I'll take care of the alarm."

Meghan's stomach tightened, and she balled her fists, automatically preparing for combat. This wasn't a burglary. This was a targeted plan, and she was at the center of it. She should have anticipated this. If she'd been smart, she would have headed for the door the second the horrible message popped onto the screen, but she'd been too shocked he'd appeared again after this much time had passed.

There had to be a way out of this. Even with her military training, a fight against someone who knew her and her background would be a lot more difficult than an altercation with a neighborhood punk. There was no way to know how many intruders were in the building or how heavily armed they were. No intel meant an unfair fight.

The beeping of the alarm panel gained speed, demanding a code before the whole system went off. All she had to do was hang tight and stay hidden for another five minutes. The police tended to arrive quickly once the alarm notified them. After last year's vandalism, they didn't play when it came to this school.

"We should have waited till it was dark." Another

voice followed, deeper than the first, twanging the edges of something familiar. Somehow, somewhere she'd heard that voice before. Meghan dug for a memory, for a face, but came up empty save the bizarre feeling she shouldn't be afraid.

A lie if her mind had ever told her one.

"If we'd waited till dark, she'd have been gone. We have one shot at this. And unless you want to be the one facing the pain if we blow this job, you'll grab her before she figures out we're here." A string of curses stampeded from the hallway. "Stupid alarm. There's no way she's not hearing it. You go that way. And make it quick. If I don't have the right code, we've got about fifteen seconds before the stinking alarm goes off and triggers the cops."

They had the alarm code. Meghan's muscles tightened with readiness as she searched her windowless office for a way out. Help wasn't coming. She was on her own.

And she was defenseless. The cell phone in her hip pocket had never gotten a signal in her small office deep inside the first floor of the steel-and-concrete building. Her gun was locked in the safe at the house. She hadn't carried a weapon for personal defense since she left the army four years ago. All she had was herself, her training and a backpack full of books and random technology. While she'd been trained well, that wouldn't get her far against no less than two men determined to haul her out of here. Into a van.

Such a cliché.

Dropping the bag silently beside her feet, she slid closer to the door, keeping tight to the wall, listening for footsteps, watching for shadows as an early Michigan evening cast weak light into the hallway.

The alarm stopped beeping, severing any hope of the cavalry's arrival. A small number of people were privy to the code, and none of them sounded anything like the men stalking the building now. None of them would want to shove her into a van or be worried about police presence.

She had to get out. Fast.

Meghan walked the familiar building in her memory. From the front lobby, the building branched off into three directions. From the muffled sounds of footsteps and distant murmuring, the men hadn't headed in her direction yet, which meant she had about one minute to figure this out and save her skin. Easing around the door, she peeked into the hallway.

The front door was out. Even though it was about a hundred feet away, it was part of the central hub in the main lobby. Whoever was hunting her would have to pass it again soon, and if she got caught dead to rights in the middle of the hallway, there was nowhere to run.

She glanced left. The fire exit was half the length of the building away, opening to the back school yard and a small wooded area on the other side. If Meghan could hit the door running, she might make it to the highway on the other side of the trees before they caught her, though the blaring door alarm wouldn't allow her much of a head start.

There was a lot of open ground to cover in the hallway, then between the building and the woods. Once she was out, the door would lock behind her. She had her keys, but unlocking the door to get back into the building would cost her valuable seconds if she burst outside into the face of a waiting kidnapper. Worst-case scenario, the exit would bring her out on the opposite side of the building from the front parking lot and, if they caught her, they'd have to drag her all the way around in full sight of anyone driving by on the busy road in front of the school.

The fire exit wasn't perfect, but it was all she had.

Closing her eyes tight, Meghan tried to listen over the pounding in her ears. The only sounds were the thumps of doors opening and closing on the far side of the building. She exhaled and hit the hallway at a dead run, bursting through the door to the earsplitting shriek of the fire alarm.

She stumbled on her flip-flops, kicked them off and kept running over soft grass, freshly sprouted after the long winter.

A shout echoed behind her. If she could make the woods and get through to the highway, surely they'd leave her alone in such a public venue.

They had to.

Dry mulch from the nearby playground dug into her feet as she pressed faster, bruising skin accustomed to winter shoes.

Footsteps closed in behind her, and then a force caught her lower back, driving her knees into the ground, her upper body pitching forward, dirt and grass pressing into her mouth. She spit and fought the weight pinning her legs as it shifted away.

Hands grasped her arms and hauled her to her feet, turning her to face her pursuer. She hardened her gaze, determined to memorize her captor's face. Struggling to free a fist and throw a punch, Meghan caught a good look at him and went limp, her fight dying.

Green eyes.

Familiar eyes.

The eyes of a dead man.

Tate Walker's grip loosened, then tightened again. He scanned their target's face, skimming familiar short dark hair and deep brown eyes that no one who saw them could ever forget. He nearly choked on nothing more than air.

Meghan McGuire was their mark? What would a hacker who was threatening national security want with her?

She jerked once, hard, breaking the connection and twisting her arm as she tried to pull away from his grasp. "You're not real." Her voice was raw, and although the words were low, they carried the force of a shout. "Let me go."

He couldn't. If he released her and she ran or, worse, stood there and vented the anger burning in her eyes, his cover would blow sky-high and they'd both be dead in the next ten seconds. Glancing over his shoulder, he figured he had about that long to explain before Isaac rushed out of the building, if the other man wasn't watching already. "I'm under cover. Follow along."

Her nostrils flared and she pulled again, struggling against him. Meghan had always had fight. It had made her a partner other operatives in their small specialized military unit had envied. More than once she'd been offered other teams, other assignments, but she'd always stuck close to their partnership, loyal until the day she walked away without even offering him a goodbye.

Right now, her fight was about something more than self-preservation. She had the wild-eyed, caged-animal fight of someone who thought she was losing her senses. "This isn't real. You're dead. Ethan told me you died. There was a funeral. Everything." She twisted her body, trying to free herself, but her eyes stayed on his. "You're—"

The fire door crashed open behind him, and Isaac's shout echoed off the trees. "You got her?"

Time was up. Tate winced and fired one last plea at Meghan. "Trust me." That was a lot to ask of any woman. Especially one who'd believed he was dead for four years.

But she had to trust him. His heart hammered. He'd had his cover compromised one other time, and it had left him close to death in a pool of his own blood under a hot Pennsylvania sun. The moment had changed everything about his life. His chest ached empty even now, his breathlessness a testament to the physical price he'd paid at the hands of a traitor.

He wouldn't land himself there again.

After shooting a warning into Meghan's angry and confused expression, he whipped around, keeping his grip tight and her close, tucked slightly behind him. "Yeah. I got her when she busted out the fire door. Go get the van and bring it around to the back lot." He pointed toward the corner of the parking lot barely visible on the other side of the low brick building, praying Isaac wouldn't decide to take issue with Tate giving orders. "It'll keep us from dragging her out into the open by the road. Too many chances for somebody to see us if we try to take her out the front. She's a fighter."

Meghan pulled again, growling low. Whether she was helping to sell his story or truly trying to escape, he couldn't take the chance and ease up. If she ran while Isaac was present, the man would shoot her before she made cover in the wood line. Isaac wasn't a man with a whole lot of patience. Short, stocky and prematurely balding, he covered his perceived inadequacies in front of his small band of ruffians with a lot of bravado and a notoriously hot temper.

Isaac's volatile personality was of the dozen reasons Tate didn't look forward to the consequences of what he was about to do. On a normal day, a man like Isaac wouldn't even make him blink. But when Tate had to keep cover and couldn't defend himself? Things could get ugly. Fast.

Isaac hesitated, assessing the situation. He scratched the back of his head, clearly unwilling to let his prey out of his sight.

Come on. Go. Tate's muscles tightened. He hadn't been a member of Isaac's ring long enough to gain the man's full trust, and he was severely testing a fragile thread right now.

The pause felt like an eternity, but Isaac turned and tried the door.

Locked.

He tossed a disgusted smirk in Tate's direction and took off at a slow jog around the corner of the building.

Tate nearly sagged in relief. Turning fully toward Meghan, he kept a firm hold on her wrist. After reaching under his T-shirt at his waist, he pulled his clipped holster free, holding the pistol out to her grip-first. "Take this." He'd count it a blessing if she didn't shoot him with his own weapon.

She stared at him in wide-eyed shock, an expression he'd never seen in all the years they'd worked side by side. Seeing him living and breathing had to make her question everything she thought she knew about reality.

He laid the holstered pistol on her palm. "Stay with me, McGuire. Just get through the next few hours and I'll give you answers." The ones the government hadn't classified, anyway.

She swallowed hard, the lines around her mouth deepening. At least she was losing the panicked-deer look; her expression morphed into the concentrated stare of a warrior. This was the Meghan McGuire he knew. He'd smile if the situation weren't so desperate. And if she wasn't so uncharacteristically silent.

She was listening. And she hadn't started running. Yet.

Tate fought the crazy urge to pull her into a hug before he let her go. "You have keys to the building?"

"I do."

"Take my gun. Go inside through the fire door. Isaac will assume you're locked out and you ran for the woods. Get in your car and get out of here. Go as far as you can. Don't go near your apartment because there's two more guys waiting there for you. Get out of town and don't call the police. We can't blow this operation wide-open yet." This mission was too important. If their target figured out they were onto him, he'd pack his toys and vanish by nightfall. Tate was too close to shutting the door on an op they'd been running for more than two years, an op that had left several broken lives and untimely deaths behind it.

He pulled his cell phone from his pocket and slipped it into hers. "Don't answer it, no matter what. I don't care what number comes across. I don't care what text messages you see. Do not answer. But don't lose it and don't turn it off. I'll find you."

"Stop talking to me as though I've never done this

before." The words were coated with sass thick enough to choke them both.

Ah. There was the blowback he'd expected. He grinned in spite of himself. "Then stop looking at me as though you've never done this before."

She drew her eyebrows together, pulling her keys from her pocket and stepping around him, prepared to make a run for the building. "You have so much talking to do, you're going to be hoarse by the time you're done."

Tate grabbed her elbow and glanced over his shoulder. "I promise I'll find you and explain later. Right now I need you to…" He was fully, painfully aware what he was about to ask of the woman he'd trained himself. "Hit me. Pretend you hate me."

If the silent anger she fired at him was any indication, this might be the worst punch he ever took.

Meghan pulled in a deep breath, her posture easing into the one that knew this business was life or death.

The part of her that knew Tate was a dead man if they couldn't sell her escape.

TWO

Tate Walker was alive. And Meghan couldn't decide whether she hated him or loved him for it.

As directed, Meghan had avoided her apartment and run here, to the house owned by the Snyder Foundation, the one place that couldn't be connected to her. She paced the length of the darkened living room, the old hardwood creaking beneath her feet. The midnight wind sang through the trees, ruffling new leaves and brushing branches against the old white farmhouse. Normally, the solitary sounds of the house settling for the night brought comfort. This place had a story, and though Meghan had no idea what it was, she'd love to find out. With the age on the little farm nestled in the midst of the woods, there was no telling what it had seen.

She might not know the past, but she knew what it would see in the near future. Hope. A place where kids beaten down the way she had been could find refuge and acceptance. The bouncing from foster home to foster home would end at this front door. There would be love here, love that defied thievery or deception, that carried on no matter what mistakes the kids made or what they felt they needed to do to get attention.

But it wouldn't happen if Meghan couldn't keep herself out of trouble long enough to finish the renovations. Her past had come for her, and no one would want a woman with a target on her back working with troubled children.

At the window by the front door, Meghan lifted a slat on the plantation blinds and peeked through, hoping to see headlights but finding only moonlit shadows.

She should have stood her ground against Isaac, should have stayed with Tate to have his back if things went south. You didn't abandon your partner. By following Tate's directive and fleeing instead of staying behind to see what happened, she'd certainly abandoned him.

Except he was no longer her partner. And standing her ground would have probably gotten them both killed, especially with her edge worn off by his reappearance.

Hard as it was, taking refuge was the right course of action. Meghan slipped the phone from her pocket and slid her thumb across the screen, concrete proof his appearance wasn't the product of an overactive imagination. From her time chasing cybercriminals in their small clandestine army unit, she had no doubt the tech in the device could track her to the nearest meter. So where was he? She'd failed him once and believed her failure had left him dead. If her pseudoescape today had cost him his life…

Unfamiliar nausea swirled, and she dropped the slat, dragging a finger along the grip of the revolver holstered at her hip, refusing to think anymore. To keep from being traced, she'd pulled the battery from her cell phone and locked it with Tate's gun in the small safe in what would be her bedroom when the house was finished. She'd pulled out her own weapon, wanting the familiar heft of her Ruger. The revolver was on her at all times when she worked on the property, but it was usually to make her feel better about the remote possibility of coming across a snake.

Her skin tightened. Kidnappers, she could handle. Snakes? They were the one foe she feared.

Headlights danced across the front windows, and Meghan laid her hand on the pistol, heart revving, ready for confrontation. If this wasn't Tate, things were about to get real ugly, real fast.

The headlights flickered three times, paused, then flashed twice more.

Tate.

It was an old signal they'd worked out years ago, one she'd thought she'd never see again. One she'd longed for in the darkness many nights, wishing he were still alive.

Never dreaming he actually was.

She loosened her hold on the pistol and cracked the door open, stepping onto the wide wraparound porch. The diesel on the old pickup rattled as Tate killed the engine; then he climbed out, his figure in the moonlight a silhouette against the trees.

Meghan stood guard at the top of the steps. What should she do? Throw her arms around him and welcome him to the land of the living? Or punch him one more good time? The war between relief and anger centered right in her stomach, twisting into a knot so tight it might never unravel.

Tate stopped at the bottom step, almost as though he could hear the swords clashing. He was taller than her memories gave him credit for. His shoulders broader, his stance speaking of an inner strength different from the one she remembered. No longer a barely leashed weapon, this strength ran deeper, steadier, more solid. Powerful enough to handle whatever life threw at him. Even death, apparently.

He looked up, face an interplay of shadow and light. His hair was still dark, though some very premature gray had shot through a few places. His jaw was still strong. But it was the eyes. It had always been the eyes, a clear sea green contrasted with his dark hair… In a rush, they brought back all the reasons she'd fallen in love with him in the first place.

And those same eyes reminded her how they'd haunted her after he supposedly died, begging her to save him.

Her grief had been for nothing. Meghan balled her fists. "I don't know whether to hug you or shoot you." She let the anger drip off her greeting. He deserved to hear it.

Tate took another step but stopped before he got too close, respectful of the new chaos in her life. "I hope you don't opt for shooting. It's been a rough day already." He tilted his head and surveyed the front of the house. "What is this place? I thought you had an apartment near the school."

"It's not mine. Not exactly." She was the one with questions, but she couldn't make herself stop answering his. She'd spent four years thinking he was dead. Something inside still couldn't process his seeming immortality and kept on operating as if this was all normal.

"I've been hired by the Snyder Foundation. It's going to be a group foster home when we finish renovating. The foundation bought this farm, so tracking me to it would be tough going." Tough but not impossible, especially if the anonymous blackmailer from her past was a bigger deal than she'd thought. If her former unit was involved, things were much uglier than a simple kidnapping. They tracked cyberterrorists on the highest levels. Small-time gangsters didn't even cross their radar.

"Really." Tate wore the ghost of a smile. "A foster home. Your dream come true. I'm proud of you, McGuire."

In spite of everything, the praise settled into the hollow places behind her rib cage. He'd remembered what was important to her, what she'd wanted to do from the time she was a little girl, shuttling to yet another foster home. It really was her dream coming true. One of them, anyway.

The pleasure chilled, wrapping her heart in ice. She'd scuttled an entirely different, softer dream for her future when she'd walked away from the army and Tate Walker four years ago. Walked away without leaving him any clue that her side of their friendship had grown into something so much more.

She was still staring at Tate, trying to reconcile his reality when he tipped his chin, his eyes catching hers and holding fast. It was the same jolt she'd felt when she saw him a few hours ago and realized Tate was alive. After years of grieving, he was alive. "Why aren't you dead?"

He blinked, then gave her a rueful smile. "You want me to be?"

Never. The knowledge he was there in front of her

wrapped around something inside and freed emotions long locked away. But the freedom brought confusion, anger and something she didn't dare try to define.

When she didn't answer, he sat on the step at her feet, patting the wide wooden porch boards beside him. "Might as well have a seat, and we can both start explaining."

Both? As far as she was concerned, this story was all his. She might be in some unknown danger, but Tate's continued existence trumped everything. His story came first.

Staring at him made her head swim, made the past fold onto the present and shower her anew with grief she would never let him see. "This show's all yours, Walker." She settled beside him, keeping a fair space between them, sweeping her arm out to encompass the small clearing around the house. "I've got nowhere to be. You can talk all night."

"No. You can talk." The friendly Tate vanished into investigative mode, his tone hard and matter-of-fact. "Explain to me why my undercover persona was tasked to seize an asset, and, when I made the grab, it was you."

Shouldn't he already know? He was the one undercover doing the investigating. She was the victim. And he didn't get to interrogate her. "I have no idea. Why don't you explain to me why you were trying to kidnap me in the first place? Or better yet, why you let me believe you were dead for four years?"

Tate drummed his thumbs on his blue-jeaned thighs. "Do you get that your life's in danger?"

"And do you get that I don't trust you?" It would wound him, but Meghan really didn't care right now. He'd been a part of a team trying to kidnap her today.

He'd lied. He'd let her grieve. And she had grieved for every single moment they could have had if she hadn't been too scared to face her feelings. It had been pain the likes of which she'd never known before, and the healing had never fully come. Now he was back? There was no way she was letting him off easy.

He winced and stared across the yard. After a minute, he pinched the bridge of his nose, then glanced at his watch. "Long story." The deep pain in the lines around his mouth made Meghan want to find a way to make it better, to take away the hurt.

Fine. She'd let him off the hook…for now. "Then explain why you tried to kidnap me. You're the one who started this mess."

"Believe me—I was as surprised to see you as you were to see me."

"Doubtful. I've never been dead."

"Fair enough." Tate pushed himself up from his perch on the stairs and walked to his pickup; the distance between them opened like a canyon. "I can tell you it's a cyberterror threat. And why you? No idea. I've been on this op a long time, and the threat's not from anyone we've dealt with in the past."

Had someone found out who she was, her talent for hacking systems and ferreting out information necessary to eliminate the bad guys? Had they found out she hadn't always used her talent for good—something Tate wouldn't know?

She followed close at his heels, needing to know what was happening. Needing to know if her past was bleeding into Tate's present. "I need more."

"You won't get it. You left the unit. When you did, you let go of the right to be involved in an active investigation." His demeanor was cold business, his voice tight. "Aside from Isaac's crew, you're the sole link I have to a hacker with an endgame your worst nightmares can't fathom. You're an asset, not my partner. Get used to it."

He'd gone too far. Tate saw it as her jaw tightened and her eyes took on a different sheen, as though she'd drawn the curtains so he couldn't see in. Maybe it was the wrong thing to say, but nothing had been right since he'd come face-to-face with her earlier in the afternoon.

No, it had been wrong for a whole lot longer than that. When she left the army and dissolved their team without explanation, she cut him clean through, marked him in a way his physical scars never had. After the way his mouth had just gotten away from him, there was obviously some latent anger stirring inside. He reached for Meghan but hesitated before he touched her, wanting to force her to look at him, but he knew better. She'd take a long time to thaw now that he'd wounded her.

Still, he had to try. "That came out harsh, but you have to understand. Information's classified unless I can prove you need to know. This mission has been ongoing, but the whole game changed when you got involved. Now I have to find a way to protect you while maintaining my cover. Chances are high you've seen the hacker we're after, and you might even know him. You're a more valuable asset than you realize, and I have to—"

"How would I have seen whoever it is you're after?" She squared her shoulders, ready to fight. Ready to fight him. But something besides anger lurked in her posture. If it had been anyone but Meghan, Tate would have called it fear. "I can take care of myself. I have the same training as you. All I need to know is who's after me and why."

How had it come to this? He'd taught her nearly everything he knew about defending oneself, while she'd taught him how to locate a hack buried in a system. They'd worked well, had been a team others envied. Now here they stood, toe-to-toe and worlds apart. Everything about it felt wrong.

"I don't know why. I was hoping you did. And you have no idea what you're dealing with." Tate dragged his hand down his face, scraping against a full day's worth of stubble. "This is not some ordinary hacker. This guy—" He stared at the trees weaving gently in the light breeze, his jaw working back and forth as he chewed on his next words. So much was classified, and he wasn't used to having to censor himself around Meghan.

She eased closer to the truck, keeping the dented red hood between them. "What?"

He drummed the chipped metal hood, weighing how much he could trust her. Old habits and their former closeness pushed the whole story forward, but there he couldn't overstep forces above his pay grade and beyond his control. "This is potentially the biggest threat to national security we've encountered since the unit was put together." He dropped his gaze to her, bracing for the anger about to be unleashed in his direction. "I can't tell you more, not without authorization."

Sure enough, Meghan drew away, her face tightening. She smacked the truck's hood, the dull metallic echo bouncing off the trees. "There's an order out on me, and you don't want to tell me why?"

Her voice was shrill, but she had to know this wasn't

personal. National security trumped all. When ops were classified, "trust no one" kicked in.

Still it had to hurt to be on the outside of this. It hurt him to be the one to shut the door on her. His former partner…his former best friend.

Tate pinched his lips together, the action radiating pain into his jaw. If he wasn't careful, she might throw a punch of her own volition. He focused on the woods behind her, trying to distance himself. She wasn't his partner. She was an asset. A woman with a secret he needed to uncover if he wanted to apprehend a hacker who had twice come close to causing mass chaos. Working this op meant keeping Meghan at a distance, no matter how much it hurt. "I need my phone. And my gun."

She flinched, the action so quick only someone who knew her would notice. Pulling the phone from her pocket, Meghan slid it across the hood with a little too much force, then pivoted on one heel and stalked up the porch steps, shaking the entire structure with the force of her anger.

Tate watched her go, thoughts too spun around to do much else. Captain Meghan McGuire. He'd been dead certain he'd never see his former partner again. When he'd hauled her to her feet today and caught sight of those brown eyes the color of Turkish coffee, he'd nearly dropped his cover story in shock.

For four long years, he'd let her believe the story the army had told her. That he was dead, killed in the attack that actually had nearly put him in the grave. Playing dead allowed him to do his job, working in the shadows for an elite military unit tasked with shutting down cyberthreats to the United States and its allies. Still, somewhere in the intervening years, he'd lost count of the number of times he'd wanted to reconnect with her, to find the easy camaraderie that had gotten him through many hard times in the past.

She didn't know he'd missed her, and if what he knew of Meghan's less-than-carefree childhood was any indication, she probably viewed his faked death and years of silence as the ultimate betrayal. If she'd done the same to him, he'd be the one demanding answers and working to douse anger. He owed her the real story. Soon. But not until he figured out why she was in danger.

Tate stretched his neck and unlocked his phone, forcing his thoughts into the game. He'd lost ground today, "letting" Meghan get away.

The growing bruise spreading across his cheek had bought him some sympathy…and some nasty ribbing from a bunch of punks who couldn't believe he'd let a girl get the best of him. At least they'd bought it.

Isaac had been red-faced, screaming furious when he'd discovered Meghan had eluded them, but after a phone call to report Tate's failure to "the boss," he'd given the group a knowing look and said it wasn't his place to deal with the problem.

Which meant it was going over Isaac's head. Whoever this hacker was, he wanted Meghan, and Tate had lost her. If he was angry enough to deal with Tate himself, then they would finally see face-to-face one of the most dangerous cyberterrorists in the world. It was possible his "mistake" would bring an end to the chase they'd been on for two years and an op that had forced Tate undercover, infiltrating the small band of street thugs who did the dirty work of the mysterious hacker in this area of the country. It was easier to get into

Isaac's good graces as muscle-for-hire in his low-level gang than to go straight for an audience with the king.

He could almost taste the end of a reign of terror for the unnamed criminal who had stolen lives, financed terror attacks and infiltrated the US military. Bringing him to justice would be a pleasure.

Isaac and his crew thought Tate was off somewhere licking his wounds, that he was doing things even his imagination refused to think. He'd make his way to Isaac's in the morning, probably to find a drug-fueled party in full swing.

He could worry about Isaac later. Right now, he had to call in and report. And, if he could convince his team leader, perhaps he'd get permission to fill Meghan in on the op. Maybe together they could find out why she was targeted and why an international terrorist had hacked something as low level as a Christian school in central Michigan. Tapping into the school's unsecured network had been the mistake that had allowed Tate's team to zero in on him. It could all be another elaborate trap, like their last mission. Or it could be a fatal mistake on their target's part.

He dialed Captain Ethan Kincaid's number, and the team leader answered on the first ring. "You safe? From our end, it seemed your phone took a joyride."

"I am, but we've got a wrinkle."

"Not a big one, I hope." Ethan was never going to be patient with anything that held them back. The hacker they were chasing had nearly killed Ethan's now-wife and his best friend, Sean Turner. This was personal for Tate's team leader.

"Meghan McGuire."

The silence from Ethan's end of the phone was telling. It was long seconds before he said anything. "Captain Meghan McGuire? Your partner?"

"The same."

"How did you come across her?"

Tate thumbed his cheek, where a dull ache persisted in the spot Meghan's fist had met. He needed sleep. Soon. But it probably wasn't coming. "I wish I knew. Our hacker sent word two days ago for us to grab an asset. No name, just a description and a location to be determined. We were to sit on go until he knew there was an opportunity. This afternoon we got a location and a time. When we went in, it was her."

"Our hacker wants her bad enough to pull her right off the street? Why?"

"No idea." Tate gave a quick rundown of the events leading to Meghan's staged escape. "But I want Ashley to dig into everything Meghan's done since she left the army." The request made his muscles tighten. Checking on his former partner was a necessary precaution, though not an easy one. At least Ashley could handle it, and it wouldn't have to go through any channels that might raise red flags elsewhere.

Ethan's wife, Ashley, ran Colson Solutions, a high-level technology consultant firm that also employed former team member Sean Turner. Ashley and Sean could do nearly anything with tech, stuff Tate would never understand. They'd been outmatched once, by the very hacker they were currently pursuing. The hacker Ashley had nicknamed Phoenix, like the mythological bird. Every time they thought they'd destroyed him, he showed up again.

And he was somehow always watching, always two steps ahead of them.

"You don't think she's working for Phoenix?" Ethan's voice held skepticism. Back in the day, they'd all worked together in one form or another; the bond formed by their small unit was a strong one.

Tate prayed hard Meghan was still the woman he'd once known, prayed she hadn't somehow flipped to the dark side. After all, she'd been his partner, the person he'd trusted with his life, the woman who he'd once counted as his best friend. "It's been over four years since I last saw her but…no."

"Probably we both need to step back and let a third party evaluate this one." Ethan's unspoken suspicions came through loud and clear.

"I'm not too close to her." Tate could hear the fight in his own voice. "Unless Ashley unearths something shocking, I'm not going to treat Meghan as though she's a suspect. If I got tangled in something, you'd come to me before you sent in the hounds, and I'm doing the same for her. I need permission to fill her in so we can get some answers."

Ethan blew out a loud breath. He knew he'd lost this round to Tate and to all of their shared histories. "Fine, but use your judgment. Four years is a long time and people change. You should know better than anybody."

THREE

How dare he speak to her as if he had some kind of authority? It was her life in danger, her past popping up all over the place. Meghan stopped at the window by the front door, holding Tate's pistol tightly. She struggled to grab on to sanity, because it was rapidly slipping, muddying reality with dreams and nightmares.

She couldn't lose her grip now. She had to face reality. Tate couldn't tell her anything because she was nobody. It was true. When she'd walked away, she had relinquished the right to know. Having him stand before her and stonewall her hurt more than she cared to admit.

Meghan lifted the edge of the blinds and peeked through, needing another minute, but Tate wasn't standing where she'd left him. She clenched her jaw, the tension in her head throbbing. It shouldn't have been this way. Finding out he was alive should have been joyful, the promise of a new chance, not conflicting and angry and confusing.

Meghan dropped the blinds with a clatter and squared her shoulders. *Confusing* was the key word. Nothing about this day made sense, and the one person who could answer her questions stood somewhere in the shadows, where he'd apparently been living for years.

Putting on her game face, Meghan stepped onto the porch, determined to get the information she wanted.

Tate stood at the edge of the wood line, barely visible in the moonlight. His voice drifted to Meghan, words indistinguishable, although it sounded as if he was arguing with someone on the other end of a phone call. After a moment, he pulled the phone from his ear. The screen illuminated the hard set of his jaw as he stared at the device; then he shoved it in his pocket as she drew closer.

He took the offered gun, studied it, then held it out to her. "Trade me for yours."

Without a word, Meghan unclipped her holster from her belt. He was right. If he appeared with the weapon she'd supposedly stolen from him, Isaac would know in an instant something was off.

She held the gun low and behind her, out of his reach. "Information first." From the little bit she'd been able to figure out from watching his posture, it was clear the phone call had been to someone above his pay grade, likely determining what he could safely say to the outsider.

Tate didn't hesitate. He'd surely been anticipating her move. "A couple of years ago, we set on a terror cell using a legitimate government contractor as a front. Their hacker would gain access to the network, tweak the payout amount and collect several times what was due. We put the brakes on the physical side of the cell and took the contractor into custody, thinking we'd managed to cut off the entire operation, but a few months later, the hacker surfaced again. We've been calling him Phoenix."

"Because he keeps coming back." She should know.

"Worse every time. He aided another cell, one murdering young soldiers without close relatives to ask any questions, then stealing their identities in order to set terrorists into their places. They planned random attacks within the ranks, making it seem as though soldiers were behind them. The kind of fear and distrust those plants would breed could rip our entire military apart."

Meghan gasped as the depth of her former blackmailer's treachery came into focus. Phoenix had targeted soldiers like her, young men and women with nowhere else to turn. She'd been in college when he'd had her hop to his bidding, had blackmailed her into stealing personal data from high-dollar donors. Anger at the terrorists caught a backdraft and engulfed any hostility she'd felt toward Tate. "Tell me you stopped whoever was behind it."

"We did." There was pride in Tate's voice, but it didn't last. "Problem is, Phoenix was still out there. He has a distinct signature, and he's fond of taunting us. That last little operation was led by the son of the contractor we took out of commission in the first op. The kid was out for vengeance, and he targeted our team, drew us in and led us right by the nose. When we caught him, he tried to convince us he was the hacker, but it became evident pretty quickly he didn't have the skills. Phoenix watched us the entire time we were working the mission. He was always a step ahead, as though he had an ear to our plans, and, in the end, the cell nearly took out a soldier and one of our men in Kentucky. He went underground for a few months, then popped up in a hack at your school about a year ago."

"Wait." Surely she'd heard him wrong. She'd had no idea the system was hacked until two days ago. How long had her past been biting her heels? "A year ago? You're sure?" How hadn't she spotted him? She was the best. If he was poking around in the system she'd built and strengthened herself, then he was better. Pride, fear and anger spun in a combustible mix.

"He'd been snooping in your system for months before we found him. We'd been scouring networks, and one of our trackers pinged him about six months ago. We traced him to some planted files on your network and had another operative dig into it. He didn't find anything suspicious on your end. The guys we sent in to do a cursory search never knew you, and you don't show up on any of the school's public sites."

"I stay out of the limelight." It was necessary with the work she'd once done. Plenty of terrorists would love nothing more than to take out a member of their unit. For four years, she'd done her job as tech director and teacher, trying to keep her past where it belonged.

"Naturally. Problem is, it seems as if our hacker found you and has been gathering intel on you, waiting for his moment. You're the only one who can tell me why."

Meghan stepped closer and pressed her palms against the worn metal of the truck hood. How long had he been watching, waiting to strike? "Why not let us know we were hacked?"

"We didn't want you to do something to tip him off." Tate didn't appear to notice her discomfort. "Intel from some other sources point to an impending attack on the power grid, and one of the few hackers in play who can handle such a play right now is Phoenix. We have to take him out now, while we have an in, or we could be facing a serious disaster."

The weight of the situation tore Meghan's focus from herself. This was what she'd fought against when she was beside Tate in the military. "How's the operation?"

"At the moment, slow. We were able to figure out who's doing his grunt work. It's a small street gang, the kind that will do anything to prove themselves. Isaac Koffman has insecurity issues, and he'll do whatever it takes to bolster his street cred. He wants to move his crew into the big time, be a national syndicate, but he hasn't got the brains to pull off the types of crimes he'd need to do in order to make a name. He's got delusions of grandeur and no way to propel himself into the big time. Isaac's prime material for manipulation, willing to drag his crew into things others wouldn't touch for fear of getting caught. Made it easy for our hacker to use him and easy for me to get inside."

Always go for the weakest link. When they couldn't hit the big guys directly, they'd go for the contractors. Security was lax there. She'd run the same scheme with Tate before, and it tended to work.

But guys like Isaac were also the ones with the itchiest trigger fingers, desperate to assert and to keep their authority. Tate was fortunate Isaac hadn't punished him for Meghan's escape today, especially with the kind of hacker Phoenix had proved to be. But she'd been around enough punks like him to understand the wannabe mobster's thought process. "Isaac thinks as long as you're around, you'll catch the flack for my getaway. Phoenix is why he didn't cut you loose or kill you himself."

"Exactly. If things go our way, the big guy may be angry enough to deal with me personally."

"Which could get you killed." For real this time. Meghan backed away from the truck and paced toward the house. The thought dug at her still-bruised heart, and she didn't need him to read it on her face. She wasn't ready to lose him twice, especially when she still didn't know where he'd gone the first time. If she had to grieve for him all over again, the pain might be the one foe that could destroy her.

"Here's hoping it doesn't go that far." Tate glanced at his watch, a chunky black monster, the same kind he'd worn for as long as she'd known him. "I have to go. It's a pretty good drive to Saginaw from here. I'm hoping Phoenix has already heard Isaac's report and decided he needs a face-to-face with me."

It was a long shot with the kind of shadowy hacker they were targeting, but it was probably their best shot. Still, Meghan didn't like him walking straight into danger without someone guarding his back. "I'm going with you."

"Oh, no, you're not." He held up a hand to stem her building argument. "Think. They catch sight of you anywhere near me and we're done. You're captured and I'm dead. Like it or not—and I know you're not a fan of the idea—I have to go this one alone."

She opened her mouth and closed it again. No, she wasn't a fan. Not one bit. But he was right. And the truth made it an even harder pill to swallow. "Fine. But if I don't hear from you in the next twelve hours, I'm coming after you. And if it goes south…"

"Fair enough." He looked up from his watch, searching her face in a way that skipped electricity across her skin. "You're a valuable asset."

The jolt fizzled. There it was again. She was nothing but a means to an end.

Tate stilled, the sudden lack of movement ushering silence between them. "But I also need…" His voice deepened. "Despite what you think, I trust you." A flash Meghan couldn't read slipped across his features, then vanished. He turned toward the house. "You're sure you're safe here?"

Whatever the flash was, it must have been a trick of the moonlight, because he was all business. It didn't stop Meghan from wanting to rewind the moment and make him say whatever she imagined he'd thought. "Safer here than anywhere else." Then again, safety was probably a thin thread. If Phoenix was the hacker who had blackmailed her years ago, then she was in bigger trouble than she'd thought. Still, she couldn't ask for help. Not yet. When it came to Tate and her former team, full disclosure meant risking everything. She'd been blackmailed in college, had been young and scared, but none of that would matter. She'd hacked personal data for an unknown entity who could turn out to be a terrorist, and the truth was enough to send her to jail for a long time if her team found the truth.

No, she couldn't tell Tate about anything yet. Not until she was certain she really could trust the man who'd let her believe he was dead, who could be up to anything now. No, she needed answers first.

"Stay low. I'll be in touch." He stepped closer, then stopped and almost smiled. "It's good to see you, McGuire. Really good." He held her gaze for a moment, then turned and walked away.

* * *

Dawn was creeping over the edges of the horizon when Tate rattled the truck to a stop in front of the small house on a back street near Saginaw. With peeling white paint, faded wood and a sagging front porch, the place was a testament to Isaac's failures. The man's life goal was to be the leader of a crime ring capable of driving fear into the heart of the nation. The saving grace was Isaac lacked the mental acuity to build such an empire.

Tate had lost count of the times he'd had to hold back his fist to keep from knocking Isaac's arrogance down a few pegs. He'd love to take the guy down for something as petty as the meth lab in the shed, but it wouldn't do the mission any good, and it would scatter Isaac's pack of yes-men to new haunts.

Killing the engine, Tate surveyed the house. Light shone from the window in the front living room, but the rest stood a dark vigil over the street.

The hairs on the back of his neck raised. Something was going on. On Fridays at sundown, Isaac ran a party that raged until Monday morning. Those parties required some of Tate's best acting skills. He'd avoided more pills, pipes and bottles than he cared to consider. And he'd dodged just as many scantily clad hangers-on who believed him to be the strong, silent type who needed taming. His heart broke for a couple of the girls he'd managed to talk to without having to fight them off. But rescuing them would mean jeopardizing the mission, losing his target and probably sacrificing his life. It was hard to sleep, knowing he could help, but the mission wouldn't allow him to yield his cover. It was doubly hard to sleep knowing some of the men and women who walked through Isaac's front doors craved this lifestyle and viewed help as a weakness.

Yeah. Weekends were the worst on this op. Tate was fortunate the whole lot of them in the house were usually too wasted to realize he wasn't.

But now, as the world tinged a deep pink, no drunken revelry filtered out to the street. The place was quieter than he'd ever seen it. In the four months Tate had been hovering around this crew, they'd never missed a weekend, never taken the party anywhere else. Isaac was too jealous of his territory to risk someone outpartying him.

To the left of the house, on the short parallel tracks of concrete that passed for a driveway, Isaac's little souped-up Honda sat close by the side door. Five more tricked-out coupes lined the lawn, chrome dull in the faded morning light. The gang was all here, but the house was silent.

Tate brushed the grip of Meghan's gun, his teeth working his lower lip. He was about to walk into the unknown with a weapon he'd never fired. He slipped the revolver from the small holster and flicked it open, checking the cylinder. Five .357 rounds, so at least they had some heft. His Glock held fifteen rounds in the magazine. Meghan's revolver gave him a third of what he'd normally carry. If things turned ugly, he'd have to be extra careful of his aim. And pray. A lot.

The curtain in the front window shifted. Was someone watching for him? Maybe Phoenix had told Isaac to clear the house and do the dirty work.

Tate tapped his index finger on the trigger guard. This could be an ambush, and the walk to the door would make him an easy target. And the whole world had better believe he wasn't going down at the whim of a pack of street thugs.

Maybe he was overreacting. There was no way for Isaac to know Tate had purposely let Meghan go. No witnesses had seen what transpired between them. It was possible the party had moved elsewhere or ended much, much earlier than usual.

But this would be the first time, and Tate didn't put faith in coincidences. The belief everything happened for a reason had kept him alive on more than one occasion. Reading the situation was his specialty, and this situation read like a horror novel. It didn't seem like this could end without bloodshed.

Tate held the pistol tighter. Inflicting pain, taking lives…these were the parts of the job Tate never got used to, the parts he tried to avoid whenever possible. If this was what it appeared to be, all of the above would probably happen within the next three minutes.

He steeled himself for confrontation, then pulled his phone out and typed a quick text to Ethan. Target house quiet. Stand by. He had ten minutes before Ethan called law enforcement and scrapped the op to pull Tate out. Of course, not texting in ten minutes would mean Tate was probably dead.

He slipped from the truck, shoving his phone in his pocket and tucking the gun behind his leg, acting as though he hadn't observed anything out of the ordinary. Without streetlights and with night still hanging on, he would be a vague target. He walked along the edge of the yard rather than on the cracked sidewalk anyone waiting would expect him to use.

At the porch steps, he took a bracing breath, all the while feeling as though invisible spies hovered in every dark shadow, and approached the door from the side. If one of the neighbors peeked out, they'd peg him as the investigator he was, but he wasn't about to take the chance someone would shoot him through the door. He frowned at the wood siding. It didn't offer any more protection than the door did.

A small sliver of light filtered onto the porch. The door was cracked open, no obvious signs of tampering. There was definitely something out of whack.

He didn't hesitate. Lifting Meghan's gun so it would be at the ready, he said a quick prayer, wishing he had a partner to back him up. Meghan had always been good in moments like this, each following the other in an unspoken tactical dialogue of eye contact and hand signals. If she wasn't in danger, he might have asked Ethan to contract her onto the team as a civilian.

But he had this. He was good at what he did, and his skills were the reason Ethan kept calling him in. Tate Walker could do the job.

Tate eased the door open with his foot, skimming the room until the smell smacked him across the face, stinging his eyes. Metallic. Raw.

Blood. And lots of it, if the strength of the stench was any indication.

He followed the gun into the room, waiting for movement, but there was none.

Six bodies lay facedown in a neat row in the center of the small living area, wrists bound, blood seeping into ever-widening puddles on the scratched hardwood.

Someone had executed Isaac and his entire crew. The larger man lay on the end, probably the last to die.

Because Tate had let Meghan escape.

He swallowed. More blood. More death. Deaths he'd

have to find a way to wash his hands of when this was all over.

He could have brought Meghan in from the school, appeased whoever had ordered her kidnaping, but then it might have been her sprawled on the floor with her life drained away.

He tightened up on the gun and focused on the moment. He had to bring whoever had done this to justice. Unless Isaac had double-crossed someone else, the brutality of the scene sent a message. Phoenix wasn't afraid to punish anyone who crossed him, and he believed Isaac's men had failed in their assignment.

Tate's mind sped into high gear. He scanned the scene, focusing on the details instead of the big picture, pulling his mind into the work and not into the fact six men were dead. They'd been criminals, yes, but no one deserved this.

He fought not to gag, biting his lip so hard his eyes watered. He examined the bodies and noted the deep gashes at their throats, quick and clean. Isaac had apparently received special treatment, or he'd fought. The blood still flowed from his wounds. He'd only been dead a few minutes.

The killer was still in the house.

Tate swallowed hard against the pounding in his ears, willing his adrenaline to ebb so he could focus his senses. He needed more than sight.

A soft sound filtered in from the small bedroom to the left. Tate hefted the gun and headed toward the door, keeping his focus on the door as he skirted the tangled maze of legs. The air felt off, disturbed, the metallic odor of fresh blood nearly overwhelming, but Tate could tell from years of experience. Someone waited behind the door.

He took one step closer, then drove himself shoulder-first into the door, meeting resistance.

Something heavy slammed to the floor, echoed by a string of curses that burned Tate's ears. There was a skittering sound of metal across hardwood.

Too light to be a gun—it had to be a knife.

Knives were his worst enemy.

Tate righted himself and aimed in the direction of the sound, but a body flung itself into his stomach, driving him against the wall, his shoulder slamming into the ancient Sheetrock so hard he went through it, his back catching hard on a wall stud, knocking the air from his lungs. He heaved in air and fought against both his attacker and the memory of the last time he'd lost a battle with his gun at the ready. The loss had earned him a knife to the chest.

Tate threw his arm out, catching a chin, then lifted his knee and drove it into the man's stomach, shoving him backward several steps.

In the dim light leaking in from the living room, Tate got his first good look at his assailant. He was small, wiry, wearing a black T-shirt and dark jeans, his face covered by the kind of ski mask common in these parts, used to combat the frigid winter chill.

But it was the eyes. Murderous, dead and locked on Tate. He glanced toward the knife on the floor, but Tate kicked it sideways under the unmade bed and leveled his weapon, too winded to speak.

There was a brief stare-down before the killer sprang again, landing both of them in the living room. Tate's shoulder rammed tight beneath the couch as his head slammed against the floor, threatening darkness.

The killer scrambled up first and bolted for the rear of the house.

Tate shook off the pain and followed, but the squeal of tires from the driveway told him he was too late.

FOUR

Shutting off the engine, Tate sat and waited for Meghan to come out of the house. He had no doubt she'd heard him drive up and was probably armed to the teeth, ready to fire if she didn't realize it was him. Better to sit and let her come to him. After all that had happened in the past day, she was probably on high alert, even when it came to him. Approaching the house with his hands raised would tip the advantage in her favor.

His hands. He stared at his fingers, expecting to see red. Despite the double layer of latex gloves he'd pulled on, the warmth of fresh blood had seeped through, a sensation he'd never been able to wash away easily. He'd checked each body for signs of life, even though the amount of blood made life impossible.

Isaac's whole crew was dead.

Everyone except him.

He slammed a fist against the steering wheel. This was his fault. He'd lost control of the situation, let his guard slip when Meghan had gotten involved. He cleaned other people's messes, stepped in when it was too hot for anyone else to handle. How had he become the one who needed someone to pick up the pieces behind him?

He'd ditched the house, reported in to Ethan and let the other man call the police. Now Tate was without a place to call home. Again. This time, it was his fault the mission was aborted because everything had gone sideways.

Every inroad he had to their hacker was gone, and they were thrust to the beginning, with no clear way to stop an attack that could cut the power to the entire nation, leaving the country wide-open to things only horror movies portrayed.

This failure undid everything. Phoenix was intimately familiar with every other member of their unit. Tate had managed to stay on the fringes, playing dead in order to do the job. Now, even though Phoenix might not realize Tate was working with his former unit, he was the lone survivor of Isaac's crew, a loose end to be cut off. He wore a target on his back large enough to see from space.

No way was he sitting around waiting for Phoenix to make a slip. He'd get Meghan to talk, find out her connection and resume the pursuit. This did not end here. As far as Tate was concerned, he'd be the one to call the final shots, not a coward who hid behind a computer screen.

The light in the truck faded into shadow as someone passed between the morning sun and his passenger window.

The truck door eased open, and Meghan slid in. The scent of coffee and some kind of citrus soap drifted in with her. "You're back already?"

Tate nodded, not trusting himself to keep the anger

out of his voice if he spoke. He needed to be gentle and noncombative if he wanted answers.

"What happened?" Meghan McGuire never spoke softly. She definitely thought something was wrong if she was bringing out a soothing voice now.

Guess she wasn't mad anymore. Hopefully she'd softened enough to talk.

Tate lifted his head to find her scanning his face, his chest, as though she was assessing him for wounds. Even though the action was utterly professional, her scrutiny made him warm in places he'd long thought cold, especially after what he'd seen this morning. It wasn't unpleasant, but it was definitely something he shouldn't be feeling.

The familiar scent of her, the fact she hadn't changed a bit since their last op together, settled the spinning thoughts that had refused to be grasped since he'd arrived at Isaac's house hours ago. There had always been something about Meghan McGuire, and having her reappear in the midst of this current chaos was too much for him to hold his silence.

He caught her gaze and stopped her perusal of him. "Isaac's crew is dead."

She stiffened. "All of them?"

"Executed." The word hit the air hot and violent, with all the anger he'd been trying to hide.

Beside him, she dug her fingers into the faded denim covering her knees, the only outward sign she was internalizing what had happened. After a long moment, she relaxed her hold. "Because I got away."

"Because I let you go." While there was nothing he could have done differently, the death of six men was still tough, even if those six men were morally bankrupt criminals.

Death was never easy. They'd both seen enough of it to know life was the most precious of commodities. It was doubly hard when Jesus wasn't in the picture. No more second chances for the heart after it stopped.

The thought made his hands tingle, and he dragged them along the seat again, trying to wipe off the sensation. "It seems Phoenix wants you badly if he's willing to execute the guys he thinks let you slip away."

The silence between them was broken by the clicks and pops of the motor as it cooled in the early morning air. Tate let the silence settle, giving Meghan time to see the gravity of the situation and the need for her to lay out her story. He wanted to drag the information out of her, but he knew better.

"We've got to find out what he wants." Meghan hit on the objective. "Because if we don't, he'll keep on coming after both of us." She looked away, chewing her bottom lip.

Forget him. This was all about Meghan. This mission was no longer simply about tracking Phoenix and derailing his plans. It was about keeping the hacker from tracking Meghan. She was important to this shadow man for some reason, and he had to find out why. He just had to convince Ethan of it.

Actually, he didn't. Since he wasn't an official part of the team, he was technically free to do whatever he wanted. But Ethan wouldn't let him go easily, not after all this time and not without backup.

"Tate? Your mind's going a hundred miles an hour. Clue me in."

He wanted to laugh, and probably would have if the

situation hadn't been so dire. *Yep.* She hadn't changed. She was still his Meghan. Direct as ever. She'd long ago learned how to draw him out of his thoughts, and she'd push relentlessly until he talked.

She didn't need to pressure him though. The tension kept building inside him, pushing against his skin and throbbing in his head. Talking it out with the woman who'd once tagged along on his every thought process would be a relief. Of course, he'd never tell her so. "I no longer have an in. I have no way of gaining access to our hacker. He's assuming he killed everybody in Isaac's gang. I waltz in and tell him I was part of his group and I'm alive, then I've signed a death warrant." Especially after what he'd seen. "We were close."

He clenched his fist, wanting to pound it on the dash until the pain made him forget everything else. "This hacker…he wants you specifically, and he'll kill to get to you." He turned in the seat, the vinyl squeaking a protest at the motion. More than anything, Tate wanted to ask her why, but that line of questioning was a delicate one he'd have to draw out over time. Unfortunately, it wasn't time they had. "I think the best plan is to get you to Virginia, and then I can come here knowing you're out of—"

"Absolutely not." The denial was firm, brooking no argument. "I don't run, and you know it." Something in her expression shifted. She turned away, facing the windshield, then back to him. "I'm going to the school."

"Absolutely not." He hadn't signed off on her going to the school. No way was she putting herself in the crosshairs.

"I'm going with or without you. If he's been in my

system, then the school's computer is all you've got left to link to him."

"Remote in." Meghan was a computer genius, one of the best in the world. She could hack her own system remotely in the time it would take him to make scrambled eggs for breakfast. There was no need for her to step into the building.

"No."

"I said you're not going." The situation was spinning even faster out of control, her tenacity wresting it from his grasp. Her stubborn nature was burned into his memory. She'd march into Phoenix's lair unarmed and fight to the death before she'd go into hiding. Meghan wasn't a coward, but Meghan had to realize sometimes the bravest course of action was to step away and regroup, come out fresh. "I'll go. You can walk me through it or you can remote in, but—"

"No. There are too many variables for me to walk you through it. If I remote in, he'll track me here. I'd rather march into a building he knows I frequent than lead him to our one place to hide."

No matter how much Tate wanted to keep arguing this, she was right. Worse, she'd never pull back. All she'd do was wait until he collapsed from exhaustion, then take off without him. Still, she didn't get to drive this bus into the ditch. "Fine, but I go with you." He hated conceding this one to her. It crawled all over him. "First I have to ditch the truck. It was at the scene and my footprints are all over the house, so authorities are going to start digging. Until we know for certain my cover was trashed, I have to stay in character, which means getting arrested if the cops find me." Protocol dictated he didn't out himself for any reason until they could prove he'd been burned. Unfortunately, proof would only come with a second attempt on his life.

"Makes sense." Meghan pointed toward the rear of the house. "There's a barn out—"

"No. Somewhere they can't connect to you. If my truck was reported at the scene, then I'm the prime suspect. If someone finds the truck on your property and starts digging, they'll know we were partners and assume you helped me."

"For now, you park it in the barn on the far side of the pasture. And then I want answers. Like it or not, I'm all in, and I want to know everything, including how it is you're still alive. If you want my trust, you're going to have to tell me why I was lied to for all these years."

There she went, trying to take the reins again. Tate drummed his thumbs on his knees. He hadn't said he needed her help, but her trust was something he craved. Maybe if he opened up, she'd follow suit. "Got it."

"And then you rest while I upload a program to take to the school. You've got that haggard look that says you haven't hit the rack in days. Even superheroes sleep, Walker."

He'd argue, but he was crashing fast. Fatigue, shock… they'd already taken a toll on his thought processes.

"I'll show you the way and you can tell me the rest of your story." Meghan reached for her seat belt and pulled it across, clicking it into place. "It's a bumpy ride. Might want to buckle up again."

Tate obliged, and the lock clicked solidly into place. Protecting himself and Meghan was going to make this ride a whole lot bumpier before this was over, and it would take more than a seat belt to save them.

* * *

After the glare of sunlight overhead, the interior of the old horse barn was dark. Meghan slid out of the truck and slammed the creaking door shut, breathing through her mouth to avoid the musty, earthy smell of old hay and long-moved horses.

She examined the floor around her feet, making sure a snake wasn't about to slither over her foot. As soon as her sight adjusted, she searched the walls and the exposed ceiling rafters. No slithery visitors appeared. *Good.* In no way did she want to turn into a screaming weakling in front of Tate Walker. It was bad enough she was demanding the truth from him when she'd hidden her past for years, first out of self-preservation, and now…? Now because she wasn't sure who he was anymore.

Tate killed the engine and sat for a minute before he got out, probably debating how much he wanted to tell her. Well, he could debate with himself all he wanted. She was getting the whole story.

When he climbed out of the truck, his eyes caught hers across the hood, and the contact made it feel as though no time had passed. They were working an op together, prepping for the next step, well-honed partners in the fight to save the world.

Meghan swallowed hard and kneaded the back of her neck, her mind unwilling to grasp that the man she'd once loved stood here now, still alive. In odd moments, her world tilted and her past reality twisted in Tate's reappearance. Her stomach swirled again, a strange mix of joy and the feeling she didn't know anything about the world. What else was a lie?

"Where have you been hiding?" She sounded like a broken record, but really, how she sounded was the least of her worries. Maybe answers would erase some of the hurt and the anger over the sleepless nights she'd spent swimming in guilt for walking away from her partner before the op that had supposedly stolen his life.

All because she cared too much to stay.

"You really want to do this now?" The slight tinge of amused challenge was one she'd heard a thousand times before. It settled in and relaxed some of the tension, took the edge off her questions.

The setting was too much like all those moments in countries too far-flung to mention, when they'd decompressed together, evaluated their missions and talked about their lives. She'd told him things she'd never confessed to another living soul. Everything except the blackmail and the hack that had come back to haunt her.

Those were discussions when she'd felt closer to him than to any other person on earth. When she'd thought, more than a few times, there could be something more for them, something outside of battling the bad guys together. Something involving a house like this and…

Not that it mattered. She'd left the service and Tate behind when she could no longer hold back the things she was starting to feel for him.

And then he'd been killed.

"Now is as good a time as any. We have no idea what's coming next, and you have to prove to me I can trust you." A sudden surge rushed into Meghan's throat, and her spine stiffened. She crossed her arms over her chest and squared herself in the doorway, blocking his escape. She needed to know how he could lie to her, how he could spend four years with no contact of any kind. How he could simply stop existing.

Now that she'd asked, the words refused to stop coming. "Ethan called and told me you were killed on an op gone bad. Nothing more. And then he all but vanished, too. I was shut out. Nobody would give me information and I missed…I missed your funeral. I spent months trying to reach contacts, trying to dig up what really happened. No one would tell me anything. You were more than my partner. And I spent a lot of nights staring at the ceiling thinking maybe if I'd been on the op with you, I could have had your back, done something to stop it." The guilt choked harder, constricting her voice. She never cried. Never. But piling years' worth of grief and guilt on top of a rapidly rising past had cracked her walls. She bit her lip. Hard.

"Nothing could have saved that op, and if you'd been there, you'd probably be dead the way I nearly was." Tate's voice was low, reassuring, the way it had always been. He slammed the door of the truck. When it failed to stay closed, he pulled it open and shut it again before facing her, features shadowed in the dim light, making him appear to be the biggest mystery of all. He rapped his knuckles on the peeling hood of the truck. "We had a mole in the system."

"Who?" He had to be kidding. Their unit was small. Everybody knew everybody. Someone selling them out to the bad guys from within was akin to betraying family.

"Craig Mitchum."

The name didn't ring any bells, but it didn't matter. White-hot rage burned her skin. If she ever found the man who'd betrayed Tate and her fellow team members—

the only real family she'd ever known—he'd never forget the encounter.

"He came in on a secondary team around the time you left, assigned to a different op. He partnered with Ethan Kincaid on—"

Wait. No. Meghan held up her hands. "Ethan's partner is Jacob Reynolds." Jacob and Ethan had worked side by side with them on multiple ops, but he'd gone deep undercover on an op she wasn't privy to. She'd always assumed his continued silence meant he was still dug in. "What happened to Reynolds?" Asking the question brought a knowing feeling, a sick sensation that the answer was about to tilt her world yet again.

Tate stared out the door toward daylight and the pasture beyond, but it was clear he saw something else. "Reynolds was overseas, gathering intel on a terrorist posing as a contractor. He was outed by Craig Mitchum and killed by a group of insurgents working for the terrorist."

Meghan took a step back, the news a blow to the chest. She steadied herself on the truck's frame, trying not to sway on her feet. Jacob Reynolds was one of those guys who was always smiling, who had your back whether the situation was a shoot-out in a foreign country or not enough change in your pocket at the fast-food counter. He didn't deserve to be cut down by a traitor. "How?"

Tate didn't say anything, didn't even look at her.

"No. You don't get to hold out on me now." Their team was a family, a family she'd been cut out of, obviously, and one losing members without giving her a chance to grieve.

Tate pulled in a deep breath and released it slowly,

his green eyes dark with barely sheathed anger. "He was taken off an outpost during the night. Tortured before he was killed."

No. Meghan fought against the horrors trying to clog her vision. She'd seen torture victims. Never, ever was it pretty. "When?"

"About a year after you left."

"After you were supposedly killed." *Wait. Maybe...* One dying ember of hope flared. Meghan rounded the front of the truck, stepping between Tate and the vehicle, brushing his hand from the hood. "Is he dead the way you were dead or—"

Tate shook his head, meeting her gaze. "No."

After all the news she'd been smacked with in the past twenty-four hours, this might've been the lethal blow. It was too much. Too much death, life, pain. It laid over her like a blanket soaked in cold water, frigid, heavy and suffocating.

She swallowed twice, trying to shove the lump down, but it stuck hard. No. She could grieve Sergeant Reynolds later, when she was alone. She lowered her voice, trying to squeeze it out without letting him hear her pain. "Where have you been?"

"You wouldn't believe the story."

"Try me."

He shifted away and leaned against the door of the nearest stall, bracing on the rough wood behind him. There was a tinge of a smile on his face, but the amusement was twisted, rueful. "Running a bed-and-breakfast in Sackets Harbor, New York."

Meghan's laugh barked loud, bounced off the rough wood of the barn and hit her ears with a grating harshness. "You?" She dropped her fists against the truck with a dull thud. "A bed-and-breakfast? Get real. You'd never go for something so mundane. You're too active, too in charge of everything. What's the truth?"

There was a long silence. Tate shifted, dragged his hands along the edge of the door, then stuffed them into his pockets, staring at the toes of his old hiking boots. Finally, he looked up with a sadness she hadn't known lurked inside him. "That is the truth. But the whole story is bigger than you can imagine."

FIVE

Meghan McGuire hadn't changed a bit. She was still outspoken, every thought in her mind a word on her tongue. He'd always marveled at the fact that she'd survived in their unit. But somehow, when an op was on, Meghan became a whole other person, focused and able to become anyone her cover demanded she become. A chameleon the likes of which he'd never worked with since.

When it came to who she really was, there was no filter. Her candor was something he admired equally as much. This woman had never played games.

He bit back a frown. Unlike others.

Meghan leaned against the truck, stretching her legs until her paint-splashed running shoes came into view beside his boots, her posture a little more relaxed than it had been a few minutes before. Maybe she was starting to trust him. Finally.

She kicked her toe against his. "I saw you frown."

She could read him. Always had been able to. It made them partners that worked. In the middle of any fight, even with their lives in the balance, all he'd had to do was look at her and she knew exactly what to do.

Of course, she'd bucked his seniority more than once, but never in the trenches.

It had never made sense, the way she'd abandoned the job. Simply walked away one day without an explanation. Even Ethan—who'd seemed to be the most in the know—had been mute about her reasons.

Still, time hadn't dulled her ability to tell exactly what was going on in his brain. Right now, her intuition might be a liability. He had to be selective with what he revealed, to keep reminding himself she'd landed smack in the middle of the most pivotal undercover op of his life.

For the sake of the mission, he'd let her into the personal, even though he'd never fully talked it out with anyone else. Sure, he'd parceled out information to Ethan and to Sean Turner, even to Ethan's wife when she'd shown up at his house with Ethan needing refuge from a killer. But he'd never laid everything out for someone else to inspect.

The setting here was too much like the old days. Like those easy times when they'd sat in the dark outside a tent or a makeshift plywood office, too restless after a mission to move out to their own bunks and catch some sleep. During those times, he'd told her everything.

Almost everything. He'd never told her the one fledgling dream he'd begun to entertain when she vanished.

"Tate?" Her shoe toed his again. "Did you fall asleep on your feet, old man?"

Old man. He was two years ahead of her on the calendar. Hardly old. "Just thinking what you might want to hear."

"Everything." The word was barely a whisper.

He had no doubt she meant it, so he'd tell her. Even

the parts that made him appear to be the most horrible man in the world.

He pressed his spine into the rough wooden post of an old horse stall. The mission had made the news once it was over, so it was hardly classified, since she knew he was alive. "We were tracking a group of smugglers who paid off workers in Afghanistan. They were loading heroin into equipment being sent to New Cumberland Army Depot in Pennsylvania. Millions of dollars' worth of drugs being shipped on Uncle Sam's dime."

Tate ran his tongue along the back of his teeth, his mouth dry. He'd long ago settled it in his heart and in his mind, handed it over to the God who could carry the load better than he could. But there were still nights when he saw the dark eyes of the man who'd come close to stealing his life, the man who'd taken pleasure in Tate's pain.

He stared at the hood of the pickup Meghan leaned against. The faded red truck was a far cry from the Jeep he'd passed on to Ethan on an op over a year ago. A Jeep he'd had to retire after it was riddled with bullet holes in the ensuing shoot-out.

"I was under cover, ferreting out who was running things on this end. Craig Mitchum was a new recruit, and he was sneaky, greedy. He was selling the bad guys all the info he could scrounge up, including who I really was." Tate leaned against the post, the scene playing out like a movie. "I was to meet my contact in the maze of containers at the depot. I suspected something was going on, had my weapon, but I didn't call for backup."

It had been crazy hot between those huge stacks of shipping containers, where the sun could beat down but the breeze couldn't reach. The light was glaring, even with his sunglasses on, the June day pavement-melting. He'd rounded the last aisle of containers and come face-to-face with a small, muscular man he'd never met before. Tate had drawn his gun, but they were too close, and he wasn't fast enough to beat the other man's knife.

A pressure rested on his foot, gently pressing his toes. Meghan had shifted, her running shoe making contact, as though she knew this was the hard part of the story.

He cleared his throat, still feeling the midsummer Pennsylvania sun on his skin. "I took a knife to the chest. Multiple times."

The guy had driven the blade in again and again. It felt like a fist, blow after blow, and it wasn't until the man backed off and Tate looked down that he knew it was much more. There was blood. His blood. And so much of it. His heart had pounded as his vision blurred and the world dimmed.

"I can't… Wow." Meghan's low voice drew him out of the memory, calmed his still-racing heart and pressed away the need to dig for air, a need he sometimes woke with in the night, the space in his chest a black hole sucking him inside out.

"A yard worker found me. It should have taken days for somebody to locate me, but he was in the right place at the right time, led right there by God. He called an ambulance."

"You survived."

Tate grinned, the fact he was still breathing a daily joy. He had. Barely. That the bad guys thought they'd beaten him was always amusing.

It had taken him many months and many mistakes before he'd realized he really was still alive and he didn't have to battle every moment for existence. "He barely missed my heart, but he nicked an artery and made minced meat of a lung. I lost the lung, which meant I lost my career."

Meghan exhaled and winced, the lines around her mouth tight. Her foot pressed harder, the pressure reassuring through the thick leather of his boot. "Why play dead? Why not let them know they didn't win?"

That would be her first thought. She hated being bested, even by him. "It was easier if I was dead. It protected me, let those guys think they'd finished the job. Fact is I was never supposed to go back into action. My place was a link in a complicated, old-school communications chain, passing messages through tech and sometimes in person when we felt as though hackers might be getting too close. I left the military, but I still worked from the outside, posing as a B&B owner. I got married, took—"

Her foot stilled, then slipped away. She straightened. "Married?" The word choked out, as though it tripped getting across her tongue.

He'd forgotten she wouldn't know. In a desperate pursuit for stability, he'd started drinking, becoming a regular at a bar in Sackets. In a fit of needing something solid to hold on to, he'd married one of the bartenders, believing himself in love with the woman who smiled every time she saw him.

But stability never came, and he kept spiraling. When one of the guests at the B&B got Tate talking over fishing rods on the river, the man told him real stability was found in Jesus. The truth had resonated deep inside Tate, bringing a peace like none he had ever experienced. Everything changed on that fall day in a moment of prayer with a man he'd never seen again. It took work, but accepting the Savior got Tate's feet on solid ground.

"Stephanie was a bartender. When I got saved and quit running wild with her, tried to talk her into the quiet life with me, she found herself another soldier to run with." When Tate had confronted her, she'd packed her things and left, moving to Texas with the other guy.

Believing himself a failure, he'd tried to talk her into reconciling, to see if they could fall in love for real and make the marriage work, but her answer came in the form of divorce papers. Tate had signed off, his biggest regret not in the way their marriage had tanked, but in his failure to make her see the truth, that he hadn't been able to protect her from an inevitable ending.

"Tate?"

"We got divorced." He dug his heel into the dirt floor, the ache dull in the face of the truth that he'd never really loved Stephanie, had been grasping for something to hold on to in a world gone mad. Now his love for her was in the prayers he said, begging God for her soul, for the same peace he'd found.

Meghan winced. "I'm sorry. When?"

"Three years ago. We were married less than six months." He shrugged, although nonchalance definitely wasn't what he was feeling. Even though Meghan had once been his partner and closest friend, it was still hard to tell her that part of the story. It felt awkward somehow, almost as though she should already know. "One night, a couple of years later, Ethan Kincaid busted into my life with an op blown wide-open and trashed my cover at the B&B. I've been on the go ever since, back in the game." He shrugged. "I sort of miss the place."

He did. As much as the job he did now kept the adrenaline pumping, as much as he found satisfaction in keeping his country safe, he missed stability.

But this was what he did. When his buddies called on him, he stepped in, the guy who always had their backs, the one who could get the job done when no one else could.

Right now, standing here with Meghan, protecting others was more important than it had ever been before.

Dust danced in the sunlight that left a puddle on the hardwood in the large downstairs office in the farmhouse. Meghan stopped in the center of the room to watch the particles dip and whirl, trying her hardest to be still long enough to sort out everything the past day had wrought. Tate's attack. Jacob's death. Tortured. Traitor.

Married. The word had almost dragged Meghan to her knees. Even an hour later, it still made her want to pull herself into a ball and huddle against the thought. He'd planned a life with someone else. Sought comfort with someone else. Shared his life with someone else. While she'd grieved until it felt as if her body would splinter, he'd held another woman.

Meghan crossed her arms over her stomach, trying to press back a rising nausea. He wasn't hers. Was never hers. They'd been partners, friends. Never anything more because he'd never thought of her as anything else and she'd been too afraid to tell him she loved him. Tate had been free to do whatever he wanted, but that didn't stop the past from clawing at her skin.

She dug her fingers into her biceps and forced herself back to reality. Tate had a past. So did she. Tate had been hurt, had lost more than Meghan had ever possessed. This wasn't about her, no matter how much her mind wanted it to be. If ever there was a time to set her emotions aside and deal in rationality, this was it.

She pulled her attention from the window to glance toward the door. Tate was supposedly coming in to crash on the couch after he grabbed a shower upstairs. She was guessing he wouldn't actually sleep. Both of them were riding on adrenaline, wound too tight to stay still for long.

As much as Meghan tried, she couldn't picture him in a routine life running a bed-and-breakfast, making pancakes and lounging in front of the TV in the evenings.

She definitely couldn't picture him doing any of those things with someone else.

Maybe that was it. Marriage to Tate Walker wouldn't be pancakes and TV. It would be long hikes and rock climbing. Those were the things he'd always loved, the things they'd done together on downtime after several missions. When her dreams for the future had turned to include Tate, those had been the things she'd pictured, along with him beside her in a foster home, teaching broken children the truth there was more to the world than four walls and video games. She'd seen him with kids in other countries, handing out piggyback rides, playing soccer and taking time to connect. He'd be perfect in this place, healing broken children.

She'd once thought of all those things. Yes, he'd been married, but the truth was, when it came to a marriage, Meghan had never had anything to give. She'd never even been a part of a real family, had never seen how a marriage partnership really worked. Her father had vanished before she was born, while her mother had shuffled Meghan from house to house with each new boyfriend before abandoning her entirely when Meghan was fourteen.

Her history guaranteed she had no idea how to relate to a man, how to give him a home he could call his castle. She'd left the army and Tate because the dream hurt too much...

And because Ethan Kincaid had warned her. He'd fallen for his own partner when he was a military policeman, and he'd watched Ashley Colson almost die in his arms because he'd let his love for her get in the way of his training. In the end, he'd walked away rather than see her hurt again, and he'd cautioned Meghan to do the same. On his advice, she'd put a bullet in her dreams and walked into a new life without Tate.

Meghan threw aside the memories. There was too much to do to be taking a swim in regrets. She pulled a rectangular box from beneath the false floor in the closet and sat at the desk she'd built from the repurposed wood of one of the property's old outbuildings. She flipped through the combination on the front of the cool metal box and hefted out her laptop, setting the box on the hardwood floor.

After keying in the lock code on the machine, she loaded the computer she'd built from scratch from her own design, cobbled together from years of field experience. It was as unhackable and untraceable as the skills she'd taught herself in high school and later learned in the army could build it.

From the hallway, a series of small creaks leaked into the room.

Meghan pursed her lips to hold in a grin. His restlessness had driven him to search for her, the same as it always had when he couldn't sleep. He'd always had a thing for watching her work. "Thought you were going to sleep."

"You know that's not happening." Tate dragged a dining room chair from the corner and slid it next to Meghan. He flipped it backward and straddled it, his arms crossed on the curved back, his jeans pulling tight against the muscles in his thighs.

Pretending not to notice how good whatever training he was doing had been to him, Meghan slipped an external hard drive from her backpack and connected it to the machine, conscious of Tate watching her every move. She focused hard on her fingers, willing them not to tremble under the scrutiny as she started the process of downloading her program to the external drive.

"What are we working on? In layman's terms." Tate slid the chair closer, invading her personal space to watch the screen.

She sucked in a quick breath, the lightning bolt of him crackling out to her toes. His hair was damp and long enough to hint at the curl that might be there if he ever let it have its way. He smelled like shampoo and... and something that would always be him alone. He overwhelmed her and brought out every single emotion she'd believed had been buried with him. Resurrected emotions had more power than she'd ever imagined. If he listened too close, he might hear her heartbeat betray her.

"Meghan?" He eased away to look at her. "What's going on?"

"Nothing." Meghan dug her toes into her shoes and focused all her attention on the laptop. She needed to stand down, or she'd give herself permission to charge. "Thinking. Trying to figure out what to do next." It wasn't the full truth, but it didn't qualify as a lie, either.

"What's the plan? And what are you about to unleash on our unsuspecting hacker?"

Okay, her work. Talking about the program she'd spent years perfecting should be easy. As long as she didn't look at him while she talked. "It builds on some of the software we used when I was working on the inside. In layman's terms—" she grinned at his request "—it will ferret out a hack and run a trace to the offending computer. Not only the network the computer was on but to the computer itself, then latch on to follow the machine wherever it goes, whether it's on or off. I've never tested it, but now seems to be the best time to put it to use."

She had to watch what she said, or Tate would realize how personal this was. Meghan scanned the image of the hacker's message in her mind. *It's time for round two.* His signature was clearer than the message, the unique series of numbers and letters as familiar as Meghan's own name. Every mission she'd run with Tate, every hacked system she'd investigated, she'd sought the sequence, praying she'd never see it again, yet hoping to track the man who had driven her to go against every moral fiber she possessed.

Round two. Meghan pressed her palms against her eyes. Somehow she'd always known he'd return to haunt her. He wanted her to hack for him again. This time he'd gone to great lengths to make sure he had her attention, trying to steal her from the school where she'd found peace. If he was willing to step into the real world and physically bring Meghan to him, he really needed something she could provide. Problem was, she couldn't even begin to guess what that was.

"How's it work?"

Forcing a chuckle, Meghan opened her eyes to check the status bar. "Explaining would go beyond layman's terms." Their teams had been carefully put together, one partner with the muscle, one with the skills. As much as he often liked to pretend otherwise, though, Tate was no dummy. He'd helped her trace more than one hacker, whether tech was his specialty or not.

"Why's he after you, Meg? This isn't random." Tate turned the chair slightly so he was facing her. "He watched you for a long time."

Meghan busied herself with the laptop, scrambling for a way to shove off the question without lying. She'd never been successful at getting one over on him.

Invisible fingers crawled across her skin, raising the hairs on the back of her neck. Tate had said earlier Phoenix had been surveilling her for a year. It was possible she'd spoken to him, stood next to him…

Of all the dangers she'd faced in her entire life, this one chilled her more than any other.

Fear wasn't an adversary she battled often, but it leaped on her with all the fury of a silent stalker, digging into her shoulders and stiffening her muscles. This hacker knew where she was, could even be watching her right now, and she didn't have the first clue what he looked like, sounded like, walked like…

Meghan slid away from the desk and paced to the window to stare at the trees bordering the horse pasture. *Breathe.* "I'd need more information. You probably know more about him than I do. But I know this…" She gathered herself and turned toward Tate. "We drop the curtain on him. Now. We can't let him kill the power and send us to the Stone Age. It would be chaos."

The hacker might think he had her by the throat and could force her to work with him again, but the truth was he'd made a fatal error coming after her now that she knew how to defend herself. In college, Meghan had been forced to fight alone. Now she had Tate and an entire team of military experts on her side.

But if she trusted them with her past, the truth could cost her the future.

SIX

Traffic on 475 heading into Flint was fairly light, but Meghan checked her mirrors again, alert for any sign they'd picked up an unwanted guest. Driving the huge pickup the Snyder Foundation had purchased for the farm had proven a smart move, camouflaging them from anyone trying to find her car or Tate's truck.

They were more likely to gain company the closer she got to the school, the most obvious place anyone would be watching for her. Afraid the dream of her own foster home would go away if she talked too much about it, Meghan had kept details close, even from her principal. Only Phoebe Snyder, who ran the foundation that owned the farm, knew Meghan was connected with the place, so no one would be searching for her there.

With everything going on, she ought to call Phoebe and wave her off. One of her closest friends since college, Phoebe would be at the house in a few hours to work on hanging the front door and painting the living room. Problem was, Meghan needed the physical labor. And Phoebe was nosy. Telling her not to come would only bring her faster.

Meghan grinned and glanced at Tate, who was

racked out with his head against the passenger window. He wouldn't be a fan of having Phoebe around for the afternoon, but Meghan needed the distraction. She needed to focus on her new dream at the foster home, not on her old dreams with Tate, even if her future at the farm was now in jeopardy.

The foster home was her original dream, anyway. Meghan had joined the army so she could obtain the education she needed, then tucked away every dime she'd earned in the military and at the school in order to fund a future home. When Phoebe had approached her with the opportunity to work for her family's foundation, Meghan had jumped at it. This was the work that gave her life meaning.

When it came to the kids, she could pour out her whole self. Meghan had walked in their footsteps. This was her calling, to lift those kids out of their pasts.

The truck hit a pothole and Tate shifted, but he didn't wake. Further proof soldiers were conditioned to sleep anywhere.

Meghan bit back a smile. He'd battled her about making the drive. It wasn't the first time they'd butted heads because "sleep was for the weak." It had taken all of her patience not to remind him he was human and she was as well trained in evasive driving as he was, something his male ego had clearly forgotten. He'd eventually stood down, asleep before they reached the end of the half-mile driveway, leaving Meghan nothing to do but watch her mirrors and think too much about Tate's life while they'd been apart.

She had to let that go.

There had never been anything between the two of them. Meghan had kept her feelings to herself, and he'd been free to do whatever he wanted. The fact that his marriage had ended despite his best efforts made her heart ache for him.

Meghan wrapped her fingers tighter around the steering wheel. Whoever this Stephanie woman was, she'd better hope she never met Meghan. It took some nerve to betray Tate. Even though he seemed to have healed, there was no excuse for the other woman's selfishness.

Checking her mirrors one last time before turning into the parking lot of the school, Meghan allowed herself to relax.

Tate sat up, instantly awake. "Everything okay?"

"Yes."

"You let me sleep the whole ride?"

"I did." Surveilling the surrounding area to make sure no one lurked in the shadows was better for her sanity than getting a view of a just-awake Tate Walker. From experience trading sleep time on ops, she knew he'd wear a rumpled little-boy look that totally undid his strong soldier image, the look that had first caught the attention of the decidedly non-soldier part of her. "We've walked this road before, Walker. Sleep is good."

"I think I'm the one who taught you the sleep lecture."

"Possibly." Meghan allowed herself a small smile as she shoved open the door and slid out of the truck. The temperature of the asphalt made the late morning steam like a sauna. Meghan swiped her short bangs away from her face and pulled the key from her pocket while Tate covered the rear to make sure no one surprised them. "We should be safe for a couple of hours. The principal may be in after lunch to wrap up a few things, but we'll be long gone by then."

When Meghan unlocked the door, Tate edged in front of her, his pistol at the ready. He slipped into the building ahead of her as though she had no idea how to defend herself if someone came at her. Digging her teeth into her lip to keep from saying something she might regret later, Meghan headed for the alarm, following it by sound in the darkened interior hallway.

There was something about watching him in his element that stopped her, made her forget why they were there. He carried himself with the kind of confidence that said he was comfortable in his skin and in his role as protector. He never hesitated, never drew back. For the only time since she'd left his side four years ago, Meghan felt the kind of safe she'd never been able to find anywhere else.

Leaving the army had been her wisest decision ever if her skin could still flush this hot whenever he was around. She felt a little bit like some of the middle schoolers gushing over whatever boy band was hot on any given day. He made her stomach flutter, as though little dancing chipmunks had taken up residence there.

Chipmunks? She should bang her head against the wall. A concussion would go a long way toward explaining the insanity rising inside her. Fighting a tremor, she flipped the cover on the alarm and keyed in her code, silencing the insistent call of the tiny device.

Like yesterday.

Meghan froze, the cover light as she held it halfway closed, all thoughts of Tate and what might have been blown to shreds. "Who gave you the alarm code?"

"What?" Tate was closer than she'd thought; his question came from over her left shoulder.

"Isaac had the alarm code." In the same way she'd done in the past, Meghan ignored the way he churned inside her, tangling her emotions and stealing her professional coldness. "Where did he get it?"

The silence stretched long, and Tate took a step back, allowing Meghan to gather her composure. She slipped sideways and turned to face him. The dim light played shadows on his face, making him seem almost menacing. He could easily intimidate anyone who got in his way...or be the man whose quiet strength had long ago let him work his way into her heart.

"I'm assuming from Phoenix," Tate said, oblivious to her thoughts. "He could have hacked in or—"

"The alarm is a closed system, and it's hardwired. Once the alarm company installed it, I plugged any holes. The system is controlled by a dedicated computer in my office, and it has no off-site network capabilities. Passwords are individual to the user. Six of us have one. Unless he was physically in the building to see someone key their code or to gain access to the computer..." The idea he'd physically walked the halls around her and she'd missed it made her skin burn. She turned on her heel and headed for her office. If she never did anything else, she was eliminating this hacker.

Tate was at her side. "Why the tight security? You training future operatives in the computer lab?"

"Ha-ha." Meghan pushed all the sarcasm she had into the words. "We had a break-in last year. Vandals trashed the building. Holes in the drywall, razors to the carpets, spray paint everywhere." The epithets dripping down the walls had been horrific, invectives too hideous to say out loud. "The kids never saw it, but I'd hate to think how scared they'd have been if they had. We lost a couple of families in the aftermath. The police upped patrols, and we strengthened the alarm system. I'm the sole nonadministrator with access because I run network security." Yvonne, the principal and a friend since high school, had had to convince the board Meghan's credentials made her more capable than any security company.

Meghan shouldered her office door open. On humid days, it always stuck, the heavy wood screeching a protest against the metal frame. "Isaac had a key, too."

"He didn't." Tate took a post inside the doorway and watched the hall. "I bumped it."

She should have known. He'd long ago mastered opening doors by using a specialized "bump key" to manipulate the tumblers inside a lock. She'd tried to talk the school into more sophisticated locks, but the cost was too prohibitive. "Who rearmed the system?" Small puzzle pieces kept dropping. If she'd had to turn off the alarm today, someone had reset it last night.

Tate shifted and caught her eye, not letting her turn away. "Since I told you to get as far away as you could as fast as you could, I detoured by and secured the building before I went to the farmhouse last night. Took my chances all it took was pressing a button."

He'd come back. Meghan's heart jolted from the adrenaline shot. In the middle of an op, with his life in danger, he'd made sure the school was safe before he moved on.

She could kiss him. Right now. Forget every reason she shouldn't.

In her small windowless office, his presence expanded to fill the space, invading the air, surrounding her with the faint scent of outdoors and something that had always been indescribably Tate. There were a few steps between them. If she closed the gap, what would he do?

He was watching her, something in his expression shifting, almost as if he'd focused everything on her.

She'd definitely focused everything on him.

The exact danger Ethan had warned her against.

Using every ounce of her willpower, Meghan tore her attention from him and turned to the computer controlling the alarm. She pulled up the entry log, reading through the numbers. "If I can see whose code he used, then…" The words caught on cold anger wrapped around her throat. *Surely not.*

"What?" Tate stepped closer, ready to defend her from whatever cyberthreat reached through the computer to assault her.

Meghan straightened and dared to meet his eye, desire for him drowned out by the roar of her own outrage. "Isaac used my code."

Tate's mind fogged as he watched Meghan, unable to reconcile the way she'd been looking at him two seconds ago, her expression carrying a fire that had hit him full blast in the chest and torqued his ability to think clearly. He hadn't felt such a jolt in years, not since a few days before she left, when for one brief moment he'd thought…

No. He cleared his throat, trying to swallow the memory and catch what she was trying to communicate. "Your code?"

Meghan's face drew tight, fine lines radiating from

her mouth. She was good and angry. Or trying to appear she was. Something had her rattled.

She moved to her desk, pulling an external drive from the pocket of her cargoes as she dropped into the chair.

She knew better than to ignore him. "You're sure?"

The glare she fired his way said a whole lot of things he probably shouldn't translate, but the loudest was an unspoken "Have I ever been wrong before?"

He wasn't going to touch that one. She'd been wrong about some personal things, but she'd never once missed a clue on a mission. "What does that mean?"

She wiggled a wireless mouse to wake up the desktop computer. "I'm an idiot." The words were under her breath, but in the silence of the office, they traveled.

Tate stepped away and scanned the hallway, wishing he could see the parking lot. He'd give Meghan a minute to internalize whatever she was dealing with, but then he'd press until he dug out what she wasn't saying. There was plenty she was keeping quiet. Her skittish pacing at the house earlier said she was holding something in reserve. Problem was, he had no idea what.

He wasn't used to her hiding from him, and the fact she felt the need to now drove a strange whisper of fear along his spine. He glanced at Meghan, watching her work. Maybe if he redirected her, she'd come clean. "You're uploading the software?"

She didn't turn away from the computer. "If it works, it should track Phoenix to the device he used to upload his virus and then follow him wherever he goes."

Anything else he wanted to say blew away, the intensity in her expression driving any remaining suspicions from his mind. When she was deep into something, in her zone, she was so incredibly…

Beautiful.

Tate took a step back, hitting the door frame with his shoulder. The wave of heat caught him again, thundering in his chest, clicking into place like a puzzle piece. Something had felt perfectly right since the moment he'd stood on her porch steps last night. Something that said they'd been apart way too long.

Something that had to stop. He was here to protect her not to…feel whatever this was. *Lord, help me out here. I've got a job to do, an asset to protect. Beyond protecting her, I've got nothing to give.* Stephanie had been proof of his inadequacies. He'd succeeded at everything he'd touched in the military, even cheating death. There was one issue he could count as a failure in his life. Marriage.

"You're staring."

Tate blinked, trying to focus on something besides the affection unfurling inside him. "Sorry. It's been a while since I watched you work."

"Well, stop doing it now." Her typing stuttered, then started again. "You're making me antsy."

Tate swallowed whatever absolutely bizarre desires were trying to blindside him. "You should show your program to Ashley. She'd love to work on it with you."

"Ashley?"

"Ashley Kincaid. She does contracting—"

Her hands smashed flat on the keyboard, the resounding cacophony of clicks echoing off the walls of the small office. "Kincaid?"

"Yeah, she—"

"Ethan Kincaid married Ashley Colson? His partner

who almost got killed?" The edge to her voice was a razor sharp enough to slice the questions thin.

Did Meghan have feelings for Ethan? They'd had some pretty intense conversations right before Meghan got out of the army, but Ethan's heart had always been Ashley's.

Was he missing something? And how come the thought of Meghan and Ethan coated his vision with green slime? "They got married about—"

Meghan practically growled. "I ought to knock him into next week."

Whoa. "What?"

"He's the one I went to when I…" She kept her focus carefully on the keyboard, though her clenched fists pressed into the desktop so hard Tate was afraid she'd split the laminate in two. "He wrecked my life with his advice. Advice he didn't even take himself."

Her assertion made absolutely no sense. Unless… "Ethan told you not to get married? Who were you—?"

Her eyes glanced off his, something similar to panic skittering across them. "I know why Phoenix is after me."

The sudden subject change whipped his thoughts around before snagging on his emotions. Forget jealousy. Forget whatever Ethan had done and whoever Meghan might have considered marrying. Her past relationship status wasn't relevant. At her confession he had one emotion. Anger. Anger and confusion. "And you didn't feel the need to tell me?" His voice refused to stay level. This was her secret? She had information on their hacker? He lifted his chin, his composure scattered like shotgun pellets on a distant target. "Why's he got his sights on you, Meg? I need to know. Now." He ground the last word out in gravel.

"I've been tracking him for years." Her voice was the audible version of black letters on white paper, and she kept her attention firmly on the screen in front of her. "I did work-study in the financial office in college and…" She glanced at Tate and seemed to consider something before she continued. "He stole the identities of some of the school's donors. He's cocky, left a signature so the world would know it's him. He used it yesterday in a message he sent right before you made an appearance. If you've got the code, I can confirm this is the same guy."

Tate jerked his phone from his pocket and thumbed through a few screens, certain the pressure of his anger would shatter the glass. He shoved the device toward Meghan. "This came from a hack in Fort Campbell, Kentucky."

She gave the phone a cursory glance. "Yes."

Tate shoved his phone into his pocket and balled his fists, twitching his thumbs along his knuckles. If she'd been tracking Phoenix for years, it wasn't for kicks. It was personal. It was something soul deep, the kind of power that drove a vendetta. Identity theft alone wasn't strong enough to push a decadelong crusade. Meghan was leaving out key details of the story.

Tate wasn't sure which was worse: knowing Meghan was hiding things and had been for years or knowing Phoenix had been gathering resources for a decade or more. "What else?"

Meghan was silent, and fury tightened Tate's muscles. He didn't have all the time in the world to wait for her to speak. Phoenix could do anything, anytime. "McGuire. You will tell me. Now."

Meghan jerked her head up, eyes flashing, but she didn't lash out the way he'd expected. "I kept tabs on him, watching to see if we'd crossed paths with him on any of our investigations. With his recent exploits, I think he's after more than an easy money score."

She was right. Phoenix had already proven he was beyond something as petty as identity theft. The alternative was more than Tate could wrap his mind around. He needed to pull in his team and their resources. He needed to get close to the target again, before Phoenix accessed his funding and something worse than nightmares came to life. "Did he ever use those identities?"

"No. I tracked. He's held them all this time. After a while, I figured he got spooked and tossed them, that it was a one-off."

"He's holding on to them until he needs them."

"What would he be waiting for?" She looked him dead in the face, lips parted slightly in the same horrible realization Tate was coming to himself. "If he waits long enough, some of these people won't have donated to the university for years. When enough time has passed, he can use the information and no one will figure they all came from the same place. He's stockpiling."

"If he's sitting on hundreds, possibly thousands, of identities he's collected over the years, he could pull in enough money in one week to finance anything he wanted. I've seen what this guy can do, and none of it is pretty. If he's after you, then he knows you found him out the first time and you've been watching. He may be eliminating anyone who knows what he's been doing." But something didn't make sense. "Why try to take you instead of sending his assassin?" It was likely, if he was about to make a move, Meghan was better off to Phoenix dead. The thought sent an unfamiliar wave of fear through Tate.

"I don't know."

Tate hadn't spent his military career learning to read people for nothing. Meghan was a strategist, a planner. They used to sit for hours hashing out their next move. Her lack of communication now spoke more than she ever could.

Meghan was still lying. She knew exactly what Phoenix was after. What was she not—

"There's something else."

Do tell. Tate waited, muscles tight.

"He's known all along who you are. Your cover was never safe."

Adrenaline sent a wave of dizziness through him before he could catch himself. Once again, the game wasn't what he'd thought. Once again, the other team had read the playbook before they even took the field.

Fresh frustration blew a whole different fire through him. "How would you know?" The demand was low, but it carried the roar of a fighter jet.

"You said he seems to enjoy toying with the unit. He sent me a message, letting me know who he was right before you broke in. He knew I'd get away, knew you'd let me go. He didn't kill Isaac and his guys because they lost me. He killed them because he was cleaning up after Isaac's usefulness was tapped. Tate, you stared down the killer and he bolted. Why leave you alive?" She shoved away from the desk, ripping out the cords to the external drive as she shut down the computer with the other. "There's no good reason except one. He's playing a game. And we walked right into it."

Tate moved instinctively for his gun. "Then we—"

From somewhere along the hallway, a door cracked open and footsteps echoed, edging closer.

SEVEN

Meghan stood, reaching for her weapon as Tate took a position to the left of the door. Adrenaline shot through her in the face of impending confrontation. She steadied her nerves and waited.

"Meghan?" The female voice echoing through the hallway robbed Meghan's muscles of their readiness.

She holstered her weapon and tugged her T-shirt over it, waving a flat palm at Tate to stand down. "It's the principal." Yvonne Craft had a habit of working odd hours, even on weekends, her responsibilities never ending.

Yvonne opened the door and strode in, her dark hair piled in a topknot, a Michigan State T-shirt over khaki shorts. She looked like exactly what she was: a school principal on summer break.

But her face…

Meghan held her ground, though she wanted to run. Yvonne was the most easygoing person Meghan had ever met. She'd hired Meghan fresh out of the army, even though Meghan's views on God didn't quite line up with the school's theology. As often as Yvonne had tried to convince Meghan that God cared about her daily life, Meghan had returned fire with the fact He'd never proven it.

Even then, Yvonne was rarely angry. The one time she'd ever worn an expression this stormy was when the school had been vandalized.

Meghan leaned forward, ignoring the way Tate stiffened as she eased closer to her friend. "Yvonne? Is everything okay?"

The other woman flicked a glance at Tate, then focused on Meghan. "What are you doing here?" Her voice was deeper than usual, weighted with anger… and something else.

Behind Yvonne, Tate straightened. He'd heard it, too. His gaze caught Meghan's with an unspoken question of what she wanted him to do.

Nothing. Something might be off the rails, but the principal wasn't a threat.

Still, Meghan slipped the external drive into her pocket, unwilling to fully explain. That would require telling Yvonne who Tate was, and that couldn't happen without blowing his cover even further. "I had to come in and—"

"You're no longer employed here." Yvonne stepped closer, hand out, words sharp enough to leave scars. "Keys."

Outside the army, this school was the only family Meghan had ever known, and now she was being forced out? Meghan's mouth opened but refused to produce any sound.

She focused on Yvonne and avoided Tate. If she saw even one trace of sympathy, Meghan would splinter. There was only so much a girl could take in twenty-four hours, and she had hit the valley. Hard.

Yvonne's open palm stayed between them, unwavering. "Keys." She bit the word off as if it were acid.

"Is this because I resigned?" Meghan fished her key out of her pocket, hoping Tate and Yvonne wouldn't notice she was shaking. She'd faced armed gunman and fought grown men with nothing but her skills, but nothing had rattled her this way, one of her two closest friends ripping away from her for no discernible reason.

"It's because we have questions about what's been happening on our servers while you've been working here." Yvonne's fingers closed around the key, knuckles whitening. "Leave, Meghan. Take your friend with you." She stepped aside, clearing the path to the door. "And never come back."

"I can explain what—"

"I'm sure you can, and I'm sure it would all be a lie. You can go now, Meghan."

If it was going down this way, if Yvonne wasn't even going to listen to reason, then…fine. Meghan banked the wall around her heart even higher and kept her steps even as she marched down the hallway, even though she wanted to run for the woods and hide as though she were the little child she'd suddenly become.

Tate was right beside her, the only indication the incident had gotten to him the pace of his breathing. They hit the parking lot before he spoke. "Are you—"

She practically threw the truck keys at him, acknowledging she was in no condition to drive. She was too busy trying to hold together what was left of her world. "Shut up." The command was tight, held together by rubber bands. If she said too much, she'd be crying into Tate's chest. Crying for Tate's pain, for Jacob Reynolds's death, for her own grief. And anger. At Yvonne.

At Ethan Kincaid, who had counseled her to walk away, then violated his own cardinal rule.

The truck rocked when she slammed the door.

"I'm guessing you guys were friends." Tate hesitated with the keys halfway to the ignition. "What happened in your office would throw anybody."

Well, he knew only half of it. If Meghan had believed God had any interest in her daily life before, she no longer did. Today, He'd thrown the door wide to an assault on her body and soul.

But she wasn't going out without a fight. "Don't worry about it. Yvonne being mad I'm leaving all of a sudden is the least of my worries. We have to focus. We know we've been set up. Phoenix is probably waiting for our next move. I managed to upload the program that will follow Phoenix if he hacks in again, so this side trip was a success. If something is bothering me, trust me, it'll pass in the next two minutes." It had to.

Tate watched the parking lot as he twisted the key. "Because you'll bury it."

"Because I'll get over it." He didn't get to psycho-analyze her. Nobody did. Nobody had yet loved her enough to earn the right. And nobody ever would. Especially once she did what she had to do now and Tate found out the truth about her involvement in the hack Phoenix had pulled off with her help. Knowing she had to confess her worst sin slammed the door on her tears, icing them in fear. He'd never trust her again, but with everything falling apart, she no longer had a choice.

"You can lie to a lot of people, Meg, even to yourself, but you can't lie to me." His voice was low, the words strumming guitar strings in her heart, thrumming against those iced-over tears, threatening to shatter them. "I know you."

He did. Better than Yvonne. Better than Phoebe Snyder. Better than anyone.

But he couldn't get close now, not with what she was about to say. She had to tell him. His investigation couldn't go any further if she kept protecting herself. "You're in danger because Phoenix wants me." She had to confess, but the secret had been inside so long, the words were stone.

He shook his head, alternating between the road ahead of them and the mirrors behind them, watching for a tail. "No. You're in danger because he knows we're connected. If it weren't for us being—"

"It's not just the fact he stole identities and I knew about it." She'd spilled that fact in the office in desperation because Tate was too close to figuring out why she'd left him behind. Now? Now she had to say the rest if they wanted to put an end to Phoenix's plan to pull the plug. "I did the hacking for him in college. He wanted the identities, and I gave them to him." The dam cracked, confession pouring out. If Tate was in danger, he needed to know the whole story. Protecting him was more important than saving herself.

Plus he was right. She'd never been able to lie to him.

Everything about him stiffened, his muscles so tight she could almost feel them radiating tension. "You did what?" His profile hardened into chiseled granite. "You worked with him?" His voice was low, but the volume pitched higher quickly. Tate never lost his composure, but the lid blew off now in a contained explosion. "You hacked for a terrorist?"

"Not willingly. And I didn't know who he was." Of course, ignorance didn't make any of this better.

"Talk." The word was more than a demand. It was an absolute order. No refusal.

It didn't matter. She'd passed the point of being able to refuse, anyway. "In high school, I ran with the computer nerds. The gaming geeks. I learned how to hack. Little stuff when we were bored. A few of the guys were into tapping unsecured networks and stealing passwords so they could get extra cash. I was into the challenge, but not into the thievery. Where could I go and what could I see without being caught?" She shifted in her seat and tried to hold herself together. "I went some places even the president doesn't have clearance to go."

Tate's jaw was tight, the lines on his forehead deepening. "That's how you got good enough to make it into the unit."

Meghan nodded, her muscles relaxing. She'd expected dread, nausea…anything but the bizarre peace leaking in since she'd uncorked the cap and let the truth greet air. "When I was accepted to college, I stopped. I'd gained direction, knew I needed to keep my nose clean if I wanted to graduate and work with the army's tech, which was cooler than anything I could afford." She kept a watch on the side mirror, not daring to face Tate while she told him the worst. "I took a job in the finance office to earn extra money." A sudden pain seized her throat. She sank into the seat and turned her face toward the roof. "I got an email on my campus account, listing every detail of my higher-level hacks from high school."

"Someone tracked you?"

Meghan nodded.

"How? Did you leave a signature behind?"

"No." Most hackers were cocky and wanted the world to know what they'd done, especially when they'd cracked some of the systems Meghan had explored. But she'd been cautious, choosing to remain anonymous so no one could track her.

But someone had. "I don't know how, but they laid out about three-quarters of the major hacks, and they threatened to turn me in."

Tate said nothing.

Meghan practically squirmed under the silence. It would be easier if he yelled. "He wanted me to tap the school's donor database and provide personal—"

"Phoenix is one of the best. Why not do it himself?"

"Maybe it was easier to blackmail me. Maybe he wasn't sure of his skills yet. This was years ago. He was probably just getting started."

"Tell me you didn't do it." There was no emotion to Tate's words. They were flat and matter-of-fact.

Meghan finally found the courage to look at him.

He was staring at her.

This was the hard part, when she got to watch the light of respect blow out right in front of her.

"I did it." She fought the urge to reach across the console, to make contact and force him to understand. "If I didn't, he would have wrecked my life. I would have landed in jail. No way out. No future." The excuses were weak and pathetic, like Meghan herself. She should have taken the punishment, should have challenged her blackmailer. But she hadn't. She'd been weaker then.

Tate kept his attention on the road, clasping the wheel so tightly the veins in his hands stood out.

Other than the time she'd been informed of his

"death," nothing in her life had hurt so badly as knowing her partner had lost faith in her.

"I'm sorry." She was. And even though he hadn't been the victim, she needed to make it right to somebody. "I tried to track who sent the email, but it was a dead end, sent from a burner phone purchased with cash. The sender used a free email address that linked back to nowhere. It's stupid how easy it was for him to make himself untraceable. I drafted letters to each victim and told them there had been a security breach." It had helped those people, but it hadn't assuaged her guilt or erased her crime. "I know—"

Tate sliced the air between them, attention focused on the rearview. "We'll have to deal with this later."

Meghan's gaze instantly went to the side mirror, and years of practice kicked into high gear, yanking the pain from her confession. The white car three behind them...

They were being followed.

Which was worse: learning Meghan had lied to him for years or falling right into Phoenix's game yet again? Deep inside, the combination of hurt, anger and guilt burned so wildly, it had to be raising the temperature in the truck.

But everything took a backseat to the immediate problem of the car approaching from the rear.

Tate shelved his frustration and focused his attention on the road ahead, knowing Meghan would keep a watch on the vehicle trailing them. He had no choice but to trust her...for now.

She leaned forward, watching the side mirror. "White car?"

"He came up fast, then slowed as soon as he got

within a few cars of us. He's matched me for lane changes ever since." The guy wasn't even trying to hide. Normally, Tate would have said the driver was an amateur, but not now. When it came to this hacker, the rules went out the window. And what they thought they knew? They didn't. This could be a serious novice behind the wheel, or it could be a deadly setup.

Well, it was time to flip the script. Their tail probably expected them to run, but the heft of the pickup meant it was no match for a sports car at high speeds.

Not that it mattered. Tate was going to take this showdown head-on. "I need an exit without a lot of traffic. A road leading nowhere."

"About five miles farther. If you hang a right off the exit, you can get a good distance off the road into some farmland."

In spite of everything she'd laid on him, Tate's mouth tilted in a crooked grin. She knew exactly what he was doing. The ease with which they fell into routine almost made him want to forget her confession and beg her to return to work in the shadows.

With him.

Because no matter what she'd said about her past, he hadn't felt this right in years. He'd found God, but there'd always been something else, another hole aching to be filled. And he hadn't realized the emptiness was more than in his chest.

Tate jerked his head, shaking those thoughts to the wind. Now was definitely not the time. He had to focus on what they were doing, or he'd have them in a fiery crash before he could execute this plan. Wouldn't that delight Phoenix to no end?

"The driver's alone." Meghan's voice brought him fully to the mission.

"You're sure?"

"Small car. Two seater. Unless he's got a buddy in the trunk, he's a one-man show."

Finally, some good news. They outnumbered their pursuer.

Tate flipped on his blinker and exited as though everything were normal, giving no indication he knew the guy was behind them.

"He followed. No one came off the highway behind him."

"How far before there's no witnesses?"

"A mile, maybe a little bit more."

Tate kneaded the steering wheel, antsy for the coming confrontation. At the end of this, there might be answers. "And how do you know this?" He flicked a glance to the rearview and then at her.

She was watching him. "Some things never change, including the idea you might need to run someday."

Tate had to tear his attention away from her. He wanted to reach across the seat and pull her to him, try to soothe some of the hurt she still carried from those years she'd been alone. He wanted to tell her he'd be there for her.

But he couldn't. She'd confessed to an act questionable enough to land her in prison, even though he knew her well enough to believe she'd had no choice.

Anger at Phoenix blew even hotter. The man had manipulated a kid, one already bruised by the world, a kid who'd grown up to be a stellar operative and an even better person whose one dream was to stop other kids from hurting the same way she had. Meghan didn't deserve this.

He held the wheel tighter, trying to keep the truck and his thoughts steady. "You still keep a go bag packed by the back door, don't you?" He had no doubt there was a backpack hanging on a peg somewhere in her house, stocked with clothes and cash in case she needed to get out fast. Old habits died hard, and when your whole life was spent shuffling, they died even harder.

"Focus on the job, Walker. He's noticed the lack of civilization and he's gaining fast."

Perfect. "I'm on it." He'd already spotted the perfect place for a standoff. "Get ready."

Tate planted his focus on the rearview and watched the car approach, calculating speed and distance. He had to do this perfectly, or they'd all find themselves in the ditch.

When the car was close enough for Tate to make out the man's facial features, he slammed on the brakes. Hard.

Tires screeched. Rubber burned into the cab of the truck. The seat belt jerked hard against his body, pinning him against the seat as Meghan grunted beside him.

And then more tires squealing and a metallic ripping sound as the car behind them veered off the road and into a field.

"You good?" Tate jammed the truck into Park, released his seat belt and reached for the door handle. He didn't want to give their guy a chance to run, but he needed to know Meghan was okay.

"Good." She jammed the button on her seat belt and lifted the center console, sliding across the seat toward him.

Tate dropped beside the truck, keeping low, and crept

to the rear or the vehicle, crouching behind the tire, gun drawn.

Meghan took a position at the front. "You see him?"

"Not yet." Keeping low, he eased around the rear of the truck, trying to locate their target.

The small white sports car sat in the field, nose buried in the gray dirt. The driver's door hung open, the air bag limp inside, but no driver sat in the seat.

"He's out." Tate wanted to pound his fist against the side of the truck. He'd hoped the impact would daze the guy enough to give Meghan and him time to take an offensive position. Now they were on a level playing field until they could flush out the other man's whereabouts. Shifting into a crouch, he fired a directive to Meghan. "Making myself a target. If he shoots, watch for him."

Her hefty sigh said she wanted to argue, but really, they had no other way to gain intel. She got into position. "Ready."

Lord, don't let me get hit. Tate fired off the quick prayer and leaned farther around the bed of the truck, leading with his pistol, tensed for whatever would come.

A bullet thwacked into the opposite taillight, shattering the plastic as Tate threw himself backward. "Tell me you saw him." Because he really didn't want to risk taking a hit again.

"On the other side of the car, near the rear window." She held her gun as if it were an extension of her arm; time clearly had not dulled her muscle memory. "And a bullet in the truck I'm going to have to explain to the Snyders now." She twisted a wry grin before growing serious again. "There's two of us and one of him. And we have the height advantage. We can lay down suppressive fire and flank him."

"No cover." The space between them and the other man was wide-open. Even with both of them firing, the guy simply had to get off one clean shot. And the worst-case scenario was they killed their lone suspect before they got to ask questions that might lead to the answers needed to end this once and for all.

"You have a better idea?" There was an edge to her voice. She didn't like it when he dismissed her plans quickly, but there wasn't time to argue. She edged around the front of the truck, trying to get a clearer vantage point. "How about we call in a helicopter and an F-16 and nuke him out of the field?"

"Sarcasm? Really, McGuire?" He'd forgotten the way stress pulled out her twisted humor. "We're all three hemmed in for now, and we're short on time. Sooner or later, a bystander's going to come along and I'm not sure our boy won't shoot an innocent." Tate tapped his finger on the barrel of his pistol. "The truck's a four-wheel drive?"

Meghan grinned. "Yeah. But it's no armor-plated tank. Want to rush him?"

"You'll probably have a lot more bullet holes to explain."

"Oh, well." She slid toward the driver's door and eased it open. "After the first one, will more really make a difference?" She slipped into the truck, keeping low.

Tate followed, knowing he couldn't keep out of target range for long before he had to put himself into position to drive. Well, he'd have to trust God had gotten him this far and wouldn't drop the protection now. "Ready?"

"As I'll ever be."

The truck roared to life as Tate twisted the key and shifted into four-wheel drive, making a hard right and barreling across the shallow ditch toward their target. He braced himself for gunshots.

But they didn't come.

The man stood and walked toward them, arm raised and weapon loose in his hand as Tate ground the truck to a stop.

Tate focused on his face, trying to memorize the features. They locked eyes, and Tate knew with certainty. This was the same man who'd executed Isaac's crew and let him walk away alive.

A phenomenon he probably wouldn't allow twice.

"What's he doing?" Meghan had her pistol raised, sighting on the man through the windshield.

"I'm going to find out. Keep him and me both alive." Tate shoved the door open and leveled his gun on their pursuer as he rounded the front of the truck, leaving himself without a barrier. Behind him, the passenger door popped opened. Meghan would cover him. Later, she'd kill him for being stupid.

Fine. He wanted answers and he was going to get them. "Gun down." He fired the command, keeping his own pistol level, his elbows tucked close.

The man laughed, his ice-blue eyes remaining cold as the gun dangled from one finger. "You'll have to shoot me, and I don't think you want to risk losing what I know."

"Don't tempt me."

"My death won't get you any answers."

Frustration dug into Tate's shoulders, and he worked to keep his muscles loose. *Control.* Situational control was shifting from power to knowledge. He had to regain it somehow.

Tate dropped his aim and crept slowly closer. "A

blown knee won't do you any favors." He shifted his aim again. "And I'm sure you know a gut shot won't kill you straight off. Just make you wish it had." He leveled the pistol. "Gun down. Now. You have no other out."

The end was close. Tate could taste it. The level of assassin this guy probably was, they could threaten him with anything to get him to talk about what he knew. Surely there was a string of unsolveds with this guy's fingerprints all over them. Leverage. He had a new avenue to aim straight for Phoenix.

"There's always an out." The man flicked a gaze to Meghan, then to Tate. "Though it's not always the best way." He whipped the gun higher as Tate fired, Meghan's pistol a retort behind him.

Then a third shot as their sole informant pressed the gun to his own temple and pulled the trigger.

EIGHT

The sweetly bitter scent of fresh coffee drifted from the open kitchen window onto the small covered deck at the rear of the farmhouse. Meghan ran her hands along the rough wood railing, calculating the time needed to sand everything bare and repaint it pristine white.

Pristine white. The way she wished her mind was. If she could sandpaper the images away, she would. It had been a long time since she'd pulled the trigger. Since someone died in front of her. Her shot had been wide and their suspect had taken his own life, but still…the blood. The violence. It would never not turn her stomach, the clamp doubly tight this time because he took his answers with his life.

Tate had called Ethan, who'd called the authorities to step in, allowing Tate and Meghan to guard the body and make a quick search of the car before disappearing when the sirens drew close. With the operation ongoing, Tate couldn't afford to risk what little cover he had left. They'd processed the small sports car, finding nothing of value. Ashley had run the plates and found the vehicle stolen, meaning the whole mess had landed them nothing but another death.

Tate had been silent all the way to the farmhouse, and past experience said it best. He'd stay silent. They would never discuss the death they'd seen today. Each would deal with it their own way, their mutual silence the one way to keep the images from etching in deeper.

Meghan dug into the railing, itching to take sandpaper to the weathered wood, to make something beautiful out of the faded, splintered mess. The ache that much sanding would drag across her shoulders and back would be preferable to the one eating away at her insides.

It would be fabulous if she could scrub away today's images and her past the same way she could get rid of the old paint clinging to bare wood.

Sighing, she sipped her too-hot coffee and let the bitter brew burn its way down, then rested her forehead against the porch post. She definitely wasn't cut out for this anymore. She should have fired sooner, incapacitating him, but she'd held back for answers, a hesitation she'd never have made in the past.

Meghan pressed her palms against her eyes and watched the swirls of color that played in the pressure. There was nothing to do about it now. In a little while, Tate would come downstairs from where he was probably unsuccessfully trying to sleep, and he'd want answers from her since he couldn't get them from their dead suspect.

Dread fused with the sick knot in her stomach. She needed to move, to forget, even for a few minutes. When she'd choked down her coffee, she'd finish painting the window trim. Then, when Phoebe arrived, they could paint the living room and maybe get the front door hung. By the time Phoebe left, Tate should be awake and Meghan could face whatever condemnation he doled out.

Condemnation that might trash every bit of the work she was doing here. Phoebe Snyder might be one of Meghan's only real friends—especially since Yvonne had stepped off the tracks—but even she couldn't override the board of her own foundation. Once they got wind of the danger Meghan was in now and the things she'd done in the past, they would never trust her. And then where would she go?

The floorboards in the house creaked a rhythm indicating Tate was awake and wandering. And like most good soldiers, he was following the smell of strong coffee.

She glanced at her watch. If he'd slept, it had been for twenty minutes. Probably, he'd stared at the ceiling, then conceded defeat. Well, he should have slept longer, because as soon as he found Meghan, they'd have to discuss her past, and a well-rested Tate would handle her transgressions better than one running on leaded coffee and sheer willpower.

It was a couple of minutes before he stepped out with his own steaming mug. He took a position at the rail about six feet away and stared at the woods. After a moment, he yawned and scrubbed his hand back and forth across the top of his head, standing his dark hair on end.

A familiar gesture if she'd ever seen one, and it brought Meghan a moment of peace. Whenever he was tired, he'd do that, and the muss he left behind had, near the end, left Meghan wanting to reach over and smooth it all into place.

She bit down on a smile, more of her heart giving

way to him. Right now, she was too tired to care her thoughts were dangerous.

Until he looked at her. Her cheeks flushed, and she took a sip of coffee and turned away, hoping he wouldn't notice. She swallowed hard, scalding her throat. Desires like these were the reasons she'd let Ethan talk her into walking away from the job. Getting too close to your partner could get you both killed.

Getting too close to anyone was dangerous. Meghan had watched love grow and die too many times, and she wasn't about to risk her heart the same way she'd watched her mother do over and over. The same way she'd watched other kids in the system do and then be left broken, pregnant…or worse.

Tate leaned on the porch rail and watched Meghan over his coffee cup. He took a long sip, then smiled. "I see some things never change."

Meghan jerked, sloshing hot coffee onto her wrist. Surely he hadn't developed the ability to read her mind. "What?"

"You still make coffee thick as mud and strong as an ox."

"Oh." She sat her mug on the railing and swiped hot coffee off her arm with the hem of her T-shirt. She kept her gaze on the faint pink burn.

"What did you think I meant?"

She shrugged. This subject needed to change. Fast. She definitely did not need him to figure out her imagination was tripping down the aisle with him. "What's your plan?"

"For the moment?" He pointed to the small lawn that ran from the rear of the house to the tree line, his amusement fading. "Mow the grass."

"Excuse me?"

"I need to move, to do something before I drown in my own thoughts." He dragged his hand along the porch railing and studied the paint chips stuck to his fingertips. "It sorts out the mess and lets me think."

She'd forgotten his quirky way of dealing with life's puzzles. In times past, he'd often wandered to the motor pool after a mission to see if he could find something to work on with his hands while his brain downshifted and his subconscious toyed with their immediate problems.

"I've got a lot to sort out." He watched her, the meaning a whole lot heavier than it sounded. "We're going to have to play this one slow. I'm warning you, Meg. You have to second-guess everything with this guy. He wields a lot of power if he can make a killer take his own life rather than talk."

True. "So for now…"

"We regroup, wait for your program to give us a hit on our hacker's location." He tapped his thumb on his coffee mug. "Not to reopen a sore subject, but you really should send your software to Ashley and let her give it a once-over. She's got a similar program running, but I'm sure she'd love to see yours, if you're willing. Maybe the two of you together can hit on some results."

Meghan shrugged. She still had plenty to say to Ethan, but she couldn't hold his hypocrisy against Ashley or her former teammates. "I'll upload it from the secure server upstairs in a little bit."

"I'll let her know it's coming." He stopped, but he looked as though he approved of the fact she was still using her talents and not letting them lapse. Then, just as quickly, he was back to business. "Anyone know you're out here?"

"Yvonne knows I'm working on the house for the foundation, but she has no address." She waved off the warning he had yet to speak. "She's safe. I've known her since high school. And until today…" She fought the hurt once again, the same hurt she'd felt every time her mom vanished. "She's been in my life way too long to be the one you need to worry about."

"I worry about everybody in your life right now."

The low rumble in his voice was probably more intimate than he'd meant it to be, but Meghan held on to the sentiment, wrapping the promise of protection around herself. She only relaxed into it for a moment, though. If Yvonne's behavior had done nothing else, it had reinforced the belief no one stayed around very long. Even Tate would move on soon enough, and the sooner she remembered people would always disappoint her, the better off her heart would be.

She forced her attention to his original question, to the mission. "The only other person is Phoebe Snyder. She comes out most weekends to work on the house with me. She's the chair of the Snyder Foundation. In fact, she's the one who hired me. And who might have to fire me." Her thoughts darkened like a cloud blocking the sun.

"Meg, listen." Tate's voice shifted, and he stepped closer until the heat of him brushed her skin. "You were young, you were scared and you were blackmailed. You've done everything you could to make it right. You've got a stellar military career behind you, and I think your work for the country will outweigh anything else." He exhaled loudly. "You should know without me having to say it that it doesn't change what I think of you. It won't change what anyone who knows you thinks, either. As far as I'm concerned, it never has to go beyond this unit, and they need to know because it's pertinent to this mission."

His meaning took a moment to sink in. He wasn't condemning her, wasn't showering her with scathing distrust. It was more than she could handle, especially after two days of heavy-duty body blows. "Thank you." The gratitude came out soft, but he must have heard it because he lifted his hand, brushing his thumb against her cheek and watching her as though he had something more to say.

His touch jolted through her, vibrating beneath her skin. Whatever was softening his eyes right now, Meghan wanted to sink into it and never come up for air again.

She needed a change of subject or else her heart was in greater danger than Phoenix could ever conceive. Stepping away, she tried to will her pulse into a normal rhythm. "You might not know what to do next, but I can give you a plan for the immediate future."

For a second, Tate acted as though he wasn't going to let her go easily, but then he slipped away and reached for his coffee. "What's the plan?" His voice was deeper than usual, a husky tone that swept over her soul.

A tone she had to ignore to save herself when he inevitably took off on another mission. "I've got to hang a new front door, which is a two-person job. After you finish your mower-powered thinking, you can help me."

Tilting his mug, Tate drained coffee that had to be scalding. He didn't even wince. "Work would be good."

Truer words were never spoken. If Meghan didn't get moving soon, she'd spend way too much time in her imagination. And if Tate kept talking, he might take up permanent residence in her heart.

The hum of the old push mower drifted over the house from the backyard as Meghan dragged another coat of paint across a window frame. Tate had spent a large chunk of the morning tinkering with the machine in the shed, trying to get it to run.

Meghan had left him alone. He needed manual labor to get his mind straight the same way she'd needed to slap paint onto wood until some of the confusion and pain ebbed. She'd tethered her computer to Tate's secure satellite phone and uploaded her program to the address he'd given her, resisting the urge to pepper Ethan's wife with questions about what had changed to make him turn his back on his own code.

She smacked the brush against the trim again with a little too much force, splattering paint on the window. After grabbing a rag off the porch floor, she scrubbed at the spots. When this was over, Ethan had a lot of answers to give her about why he'd steered her away from Tate while popping the question to Ashley.

Meghan rolled her shoulders, trying to shake off the tension, then slipped her brush into the pail to reload. She paused at the smooth purr of an engine. Setting the brush aside, she turned slowly, not touching her gun but mentally measuring how long it would take to reach it. The thought of using it again curled her insides.

Phoebe Snyder's silver luxury sedan glided to a stop near the porch.

Meghan relaxed. So far, no one had shown any indication that they knew Tate and Meghan were here, so it was safe for Phoebe to drop by. Telling her not to come would raise more red flags than letting her follow her routine as usual.

Besides, Phoebe was a safe intrusion who brought some much-needed distraction. The pair had been close since they'd met freshman year at Michigan State, and Meghan had stood by Phoebe when her marine brother was killed in a friendly fire incident overseas. Phoebe had drifted for a while, grieving for her brother with fierce anger that had divided their friendship, but they'd reunited almost two years ago when Phoebe found her bearings and started the foundation to foster kids through difficult times in memory of her brother.

Meghan counted Phoebe as the sister she'd never had. Her father owned a plant that made engine components for the auto industry. Through some savvy business practices, Snyder Industries had weathered the migration of factories to other countries, remaining profitable enough to fund the foundation Phoebe had started. Relieved to see his daughter overcome her grief, Clinton Snyder had been more than willing to finance her dream.

Phoebe slid out of the car, decked out in paint-stained blue jeans and a shirt from a college fun run, her ponytail straggling blond tendrils around her makeup-free face. Her presence was what Meghan needed to soothe the last of her pain. She'd embrace Phoebe's friendship for as long as the other girl offered it.

Phoebe tossed her a wave as she pulled two huge plastic bags from the trunk, hefting her home improvement haul to the porch. "You've been busy this morning."

A galactic understatement. "Decided to get moving

on the outside. The sooner we get done, the faster we get the kids here."

"You got that right. The trim turned out amazing. I'll dump this inside, and we can start on the living room. Or we can finish out here. I'm ready for anything." Phoebe stopped at the steps and tilted her head, arching one perfect eyebrow. "Is someone mowing the grass?"

Meghan took one of the bags from Phoebe and accepted a side-armed hug. "An old army buddy showed up to help for a day or two." No need for specifics. When Phoebe had come back into her life, Meghan had spilled her heart over late-night Chinese food, pouring out her feelings about Tate, the man she'd believed to be long buried. Explaining to Phoebe why a dead man was mowing the grass would be complicated at best and would violate national security at worst. Instead, she shoved hair out of her eyes with her forearm and opened the front door. "If you come in the kitchen, I've got coffee ready and I'll show you what I did last weekend."

"Tell me you didn't lay all of the tile by yourself."

Meghan grinned and dropped the bag by the door. "I won't."

"I told you to wait for me to help. How long did it take you?" Following Meghan's lead, she propped her bag beside the other and rotated her wrist.

"The whole weekend. I needed physical labor after closing out the year at the school. Sitting behind a computer too long makes me long for construction." Stopping at the kitchen door, Meghan swept her arm into the room, proud of her work on the faux redbrick tile.

Phoebe clapped her hands. "I love it. I wasn't sure when you first suggested it, but with the huge stone fireplace in the corner, the kids are going to think they live in a pizzeria." She grinned at the floor, then walked to the window to peek out. "Maybe we should paint the walls red or something."

Meghan tried to see the room through a different lens. The kitchen did kind of remind her of an old-school pizza parlor. "Might be fun to do something a little bit different, give the kids something to make them feel special."

"It's a thought." Phoebe's voice was distracted, as if she hadn't heard a word. She glanced at Meghan over her shoulder. "That's your army buddy? When you said someone was here, I assumed a woman. He's no woman. And he's cute, if you're fond of the type." She turned to the window. "And by type I mean built. Wow."

Meghan peeked over Phoebe's shoulder and tried to see Tate through the other woman's lens. He was toned, like a guy who'd spent his life using his muscles for manual labor. She'd always thought of him as the outdoor type, the kind who earned his build through hard work, not sweating it out in an armless T-shirt at the gym. "If you say so." Although she really wished Phoebe wouldn't say so.

She swiped the sheer white curtain out of Phoebe's grasp, swinging it over the window, the desire to talk dying in a green haze. Tate wasn't just any guy to be ogling. He was...Tate. And in some bizarre way, he was hers. She'd never had to share him.

Well, obviously, he'd once belonged to someone else, a fact that still sat oddly. But the idea of anyone sizing him up as if he were Mr. January? It seemed wrong. In about six hundred different ways.

Phoebe watched her, amused gaze bouncing from Meghan to the curtained window. "Is there a story here

I've never heard? And it must be a good one, because I'm pretty sure I've heard all of your stories, and other than what you told me about the guy who died, none of them involved a man like the one mowing our grass right now."

Meghan fingered the hem of her T-shirt. She wasn't going to lie, but she also wasn't going to blow Tate's cover, not even to Phoebe. "No story. It was the army. I worked with a lot of guys. He was a buddy a long time ago."

"Who showed up out of nowhere all of a sudden." Phoebe's look was knowing, teasing. "Did he come after you or did you track him down?"

A headache throbbed behind Meghan's right temple, a combination of exhaustion and the twisted stories she had to keep straight. "We ran into each other yesterday, and he needed a place to crash. There's nothing more to it."

Phoebe hip-checked Meghan, her grin widening. "Don't worry, hon. I have no interest in him. I was merely pointing out what you already saw." She winked and headed through the den. "Know what? Let's paint. You can introduce me to your friend later. Or maybe I should give you a makeover and let him see—"

"He's here for a day. Get your mind out of those romance novels you bury your nose in. He's not the drifter who's going to come in and sweep me off my feet." No, he'd done the sweeping a long time ago. Then he'd died, led an entire other life. The usual stuff that got in the way of true love.

Meghan needed to remember her place, anyway. She was here for the kids, not to trap a husband. "Let's grab the paint and get started on the living room."

"Fine." Phoebe's sigh was as long suffering as they came. "Where is it?"

Meghan stopped short, reading her to-do list in her mind. Paint wasn't her task. It was Phoebe's. "I assumed it was in your car. Paint was your job. When you got the supplies you were supposed to get the paint we preordered?"

Phoebe's shoulders slumped. "No. Really?"

"Yes. Really." Meghan stepped between Phoebe and the front door, trying to catch her attention. This was far from the first time Phoebe had let something slip right past her. She wasn't a ditz, but she was married to her to-do list. Without it, her world spun out of orbit. "I knew I should have texted to remind you." Meghan grinned.

Phoebe didn't. Instead, a haunted look crossed her face, and she frowned. "Great. There's a lot going on with the house needing to be ready and my dad breathing down my neck about it. It's the first responsibility he's let me really handle, and he's not sure he trusts me after the way I acted after Robert was killed." She sighed and shrugged off whatever she was thinking. "Know what? I'll be back in a couple of hours. It shouldn't take long to—"

"Wait." Meghan grabbed Phoebe's elbow. Maybe this was the way to keep her out of harm's way until this mess straightened out. "I've got enough to do here without you running back and forth. Bring it after church tomorrow and we'll start then."

"You're sure?"

"Yeah." At this point, the idea of introducing Tate to Phoebe was growing more uncomfortable by the second. It was easier if they didn't meet at all.

Phoebe pulled away, stepped around Meghan and was across the yard without offering another word.

Watching the car disappear around the bend in the drive, Meghan narrowed her eyes. One skill she'd learned in the army was how to read people, and there was one thing for certain. Phoebe was not herself. And as soon as things leveled off, Meghan was going to find out why.

NINE

For the first time in his professional life, Tate had no answers. He wiped his face on the hem of his T-shirt and surveyed the small lawn. It had taken less than an hour to mow, just as Meghan had predicted. Not nearly enough time to erase the horrors of the day or to devise any answers, but plenty of time to generate a restlessness that grew with every step behind the protesting old gas push mower Meghan had dug out of the barn.

He missed the manual push mower at the bed-and-breakfast. It had required force to get it moving, exertion to keep it going. And the lawn at the place had been huge. Even though it was tucked in a neighborhood near the harbor, the lawn's square footage was phenomenal. The physical activity required to keep the B&B up to par had been enough to untangle many knots. It had kept him sane after Stephanie left him, enabling him to get exercise while his heart prayed for direction. The yard had given him time to grow his relationship with the God who now guided his life, time to realize how much a marriage without equal faith could destroy a man when his wife wanted to keep driving her life down a dangerous path.

A cloud of gnats scattered as he swiped them from his face. Tate hadn't had his own yard to mow in more than a year, not since a crew of armed men kicked in his door, gunning for Ethan and Ashley, who'd taken refuge there from a terror cell. Sometimes it seemed his whole life was dictated by people who wanted him dead.

He brushed the mower's grip, the cracked rubber rough under his touch. This was what he did. He protected. He stuck close to the shadows so he could step in and have other peoples' backs. The team needed him. And he needed them, because he had no idea who he'd be without a mission to guide him.

He turned the mower and headed for the shed at the corner of the house. Still, stability would be nice. A life without terrorists, executions and public suicides. Some days, it would be nice to go to bed at night knowing tomorrow would be routine and boring.

It didn't help that every step behind the stinking mower had jarred loose another memory about Meghan. Good memories, all. Memories he'd forgotten…or shoved aside. Being here made him feel alive for the first time since the knife had entered his chest.

He stopped walking. *No.* For the first time since he'd arrived at work on a Wednesday morning to find her gone.

Worse, every time they were in close proximity, his response to her grew. It had been building all day, the need to stand a little closer, to touch her. And on the porch earlier? To kiss her until she made the memories disappear.

Always, though, the mission stood in the way. She was his to protect, not his to fall in love with. Until

Phoenix was locked away, all he could offer her was an uncertain future with no safe place to land.

"Finished already?" Meghan appeared at the corner of the house in paint-stained jeans and an old gray army T-shirt. Her short dark hair was pushed back in a headband, and she looked the exact same as she had on their last op together. Young. Beautiful. The picture of wide-eyed innocence.

The facade of innocence made even the hardest of criminals trust her...and underestimate her. It was a facade she'd carefully cultivated. Meghan had fought more in her childhood than most people would in a lifetime, and she'd battled back to win every time. He admired her in a way he'd never admired another human being. Her strength. Her tenacity. Her sheer bravery in the face of everything from armed terrorists to camel spiders.

Tate quirked a half grin. The one thing she cringed at was snakes. He'd relished every time he'd been able to step in and protect her from slithering serpents. Made him feel bigger, as though she needed him a little bit. As though he could spend his life making sure she never had to fight off anything again.

Flipping his hand in front of his face, he swiped the gnats and the thought away. She was his former partner, and any affection he'd ever percolated for her didn't matter. She was married to her job, and the only thing Tate was any good at was his. He'd learned that the hard way.

"Hey." Meghan waved her arms over her head. "You asleep on your feet? I told you to catch some rack time."

"Whatever." He shoved everything else aside and

leaned heavily on the mower, the weight of his world magnifying gravity.

"I asked if you're finished."

"Yeah." He glanced over his shoulder at the old horse pasture, barely visible on the other side of the trees. If she had a bigger mower—

"Don't even think about it." There was laughter in her voice. "You'd kill yourself trying to tame the weeds. I don't want to haul you to the hospital with heat exhaustion because you're a stubborn old soldier."

He turned to her. Sure enough, she was smiling, the gleam in her eye familiar and new all at the same time. She knew him. Knew exactly what he was thinking, and she called him to reality when he was out of line. Just as if they'd never stopped working together. Just the way he needed someone to do.

He scrubbed his cheek, rough with too many days' worth of stubble. Man, he was past exhausted if he was losing control of his emotions this way. Maybe he should have listened to her and caught a power nap.

Not that he'd ever tell her she was right.

"You puzzle out anything while you were out here sweating to death?" She stepped closer, holding out a large glass of ice water, condensation dripping down the sides.

"I figured out I miss mowing grass, and Michigan summers are hotter than the rest of the world gives them credit for. But I didn't figure out this mission, other than I need to take you to—"

"No." She hadn't wavered a bit on letting him take her to headquarters where it was safe. "And June is rarely this hot. But I'll tell you what. After you finish your water, you can help me hang the front door.

Phoebe came by, but she won't be back till tomorrow. I'd love to have the door hung today so the gnats will stop sneaking in around the cracks."

Someone had come and gone and he'd missed it? Meghan had warned him Phoebe would be there, which meant he should have been watching for her arrival, but somehow, in his grass-mowing haze, he'd lost focus. "You trust her?"

"I've known her since my first day at college. She walked into my dorm room thinking it was hers." Meghan smiled a quick smile, one of the few truly joyful ones he'd ever seen on her. "Turned out she was in the whole wrong building."

Tate tightened his jaw. With the story she'd told him, it was probable their hacker tracked her out of high school. A friend she'd met in college wasn't much of a threat, but he still wasn't a fan of someone else knowing he was on the property, of someone else having access to Meghan, not when their hacker was a ghost and he had no way of knowing who Meghan's link to him was.

"What?" She shook her head, watching his thoughts play out on his face. "I get it. You're suspicious, but there comes a time when you have to make the decision to trust. I trust Phoebe."

The way you trusted Yvonne? Nope. Can't say that. Rather than set off her temper, he swigged ice water, letting the cold hit the roof of his mouth and seep down his throat, sparking the same sensation shoveling in grape shaved ice too fast as a kid did. He held the empty glass out to her and pressed his tongue to the roof of his mouth, trying to ease the ache.

She took the glass and held it loosely by her side. "Help me hang the door, and I'll show you where the weed whacker is. Maybe you can think some more while you attack the pests growing on the side of the house." She jerked her thumb over her shoulder, then turned to walk away. "New door's in the shed. I painted it last week, but hanging it is a two-person job."

"Getting soft in your civilian life, McGuire?" And bossy, but that was another observation he'd keep to himself.

She tossed a saucy smirk over her shoulder. "Spoken like a man who has never tried to corral a room full of middle schoolers on the day before Christmas break."

"You've got me there." Tate watched the patch of grass directly in front of the mower. Something about her sass was too much, with the rug already jerked out from under his life. "You going to miss school?"

"Maybe." Her pace didn't slow, and Tate looked up to find himself staring at the short, spiky hair at the back of her head. "No. I'll have plenty to keep me busy here. Some of the harder cases, they'll need to be tutored to gain the academic ground they've lost. My experience comes into play there."

"Along with tracking them through the woods if they run away." He caught up with her and pushed the mower along beside her, trying not to watch her face too intently.

She laughed. "If it comes to that." She sobered quickly. "I really hope it doesn't come to that. I hope..." She stopped, fixed on something across the driveway, on the other side of the small shed where the prepped front door waited. "I hope they're happy enough, loved enough, to stay."

There was a wistfulness in her voice. She knew the truth as well as he did. Some would stay. And some would do their level best to push every button Meghan had. Some would accept love and flourish. Some never would, and only God knew what would happen when they left this place of last chances.

Tate started to speak, then realized he had nothing of value to say. Her passion was contagious, though. What would it be like to make a difference to a kid who needed love?

Tate pushed the mower across the dirt driveway, wishing he had something to contribute. Back in the day it had been easy, but they'd shared so much then. Now she walked beside him, practically a stranger, even though her appearance was the same as his old partner's, she walked and talked the same as his old partner and she gave him attitude the same as his old partner.

His smile flared, then faded. Separate experiences had changed them, and no matter how much they still knew about each other, the divergence in their lives left them an unsettling kind of familiar strangers.

Tate didn't like it. He didn't like one single thing happening in his life right now.

Except for Meghan.

He looked over his shoulder at the pasture again. It would take two days or more to mow, but maybe if he started now, he'd have everything prayed out by the time he was finished.

If he never hung another door again, it would be too soon. For the rest of his life, Tate would never take for granted a barrier between him and the outside world. As much as he loved physical labor, this was the biggest beast he'd ever tamed.

Meghan sat on her heels in the open doorway, safety

goggles in place and a cordless drill in her hand. She wielded it with as much practice as she'd once wielded her pistol.

Her confidence shouldn't have made him want to sit and watch her work. Although he could. Contentedly. For the rest of the day.

He needed to think of something else fast, or he might settle in and watch to his heart's content. Tate swiped at his forehead with the back of his wrist, sawdust and grit scrubbing his skin, watching her secure a screw in the strike plate. "How did you get so good at home improvements?"

She waited for the drill to stop whirring. "Somebody had to do it, and I was in a position to take the lead. I went to the home improvement store and had them teach me everything I needed to know." She held her hand out for another screw, and he dropped it into her palm. "Everything you see inside is me, with a little help from Phoebe and a few volunteers. It's been good therapy."

Tate leaned against the wood siding, giving in to the temptation to watch her. At first, he'd tried to step in and do the heavy lifting, but he saw the way the wind blew. She only wanted him as a gofer.

Fine. It was her house, even though he itched to grab a hammer, a drill, something to make himself useful. But he'd been right earlier. Watching her was almost as much fun. "Therapy? What were you trying to get over?"

The drill stopped whirring, the screw halfway set. Meghan stared at it, as though she'd forgotten what to do.

Tate squatted beside her, knees cracking in protest after standing for so long. "What's going on?"

"Nothing." She came back from far away, driving the screw in as if it had attacked her.

Tate arched an eyebrow. When she held out her hand for another screw, he closed his fingers around the ones he held, refusing to pass one over. "You wouldn't let me keep quiet earlier. I'm returning the favor."

Her open palm never wavered. "Knock it off, Walker. The sooner this door is in, the sooner I can turn on the air-conditioning."

It was tempting, but so was learning her secret. "You forget I've slogged months through the desert. Michigan heat waves don't scare me." Although being this close to Meghan ranked up there.

She pursed her lips, the corner twitching into a smile that didn't quite reach her eyes. "I was getting over how bossy my partner was."

"Whatever." He dropped the screw into her palm, letting her make the joke. Sooner or later, she'd talk. She always did.

After testing the security of the strike plate, Meghan propped her wrists on her knees and let her hands dangle. "Done." She pivoted to stand.

Tate reached out to pull her up, but she held out the drill to him instead. She pulled the door shut, checking the perimeter, then opened it again. "Let's get this mess cleared, then I think dialing the AC to fifty will be good."

Cold sounded like the best relief in the world. Cold and a shower. Between mowing the yard and fitting the door, Tate's skin was a plaster of sawdust and dirt. He leaned over and hooked the handles on a small plastic bag.

The window above him shattered, raining glass into the house.

"Tate!" Meghan scrambled toward him as the gunshot's echo died.

He didn't hesitate, but raised enough to grab her around the waist and shove her into the house as a thud hit the siding and another gunshot ricocheted off the trees. "Get into the kitchen." He pushed her toward the other room, desperate to get her out of harm's way, chest aching from the adrenaline jolt.

She fought, breaking free. "I'm not leaving you to fight alone." Meghan dropped behind the couch, grabbing his arm to bring him with her. Back pressed against the sofa, she checked her ammo while he pulled his gun from its holster. She glanced at him grimly, fire behind her eyes. "Just like old times."

"You're not half as funny as you think you are." He jabbed a finger toward the kitchen. "You need to take cover." If anything happened to her...

"And you—"

Another shot pinged off metal, echoing across the trees.

Meghan winced. "My car."

"Or the pickup. We left it in the driveway." He turned toward the kitchen, calculating the distance they'd have to run to the trees, where they could skirt through cover to make it to around the pasture. "Think we can get to mine in the barn?"

Meghan nodded, scanning the wall as though she could see through it. "There's a trail from the barn to the main road if your clunker has four-wheel drive."

"It does, but I can't guarantee it will work."

"It'd better." She swiped her hair from her face. "Shooting stopped."

The silence was thick, more ominous than gunshots. Their attacker was probably creeping closer to the house.

They were safe if they could get out the back. And if the gunman was alone. How likely was it they'd been flanked and someone was waiting in the trees?

Even more pertinent, how had they been found in the first place?

The window on the far side of the door shattered, the gunshot's crack closer this time.

No way was he going to sit here while some coward took potshots at them from a distance. No one got to pin them down. He leaned forward. "We've got two options. Wait for him to come through the door and pray we get a shot off first, or get out now."

"I prefer option two, but then none of our questions get answered. He might know where we are, but we know where he is, too. I promise you he knows a lot more than we do."

She was right. Answers lay on the other side of a sniper's rifle. If they left, they abandoned any chance of asking the questions. But if they stayed, they might be facing God in heaven and getting every answer they ever wanted long before they wanted them.

The idea of confronting the hacker who'd shadowed almost two years of his life was more than he could turn his back on. Whoever was shooting at them now could lead them straight to Phoenix and close this whole operation.

Tate peeked around the couch. The silence crawled along his arms. "I understand how the cat died now."

"What?"

"Curiosity." Tate turned and rested on one knee, fired two shots over the couch through the already shattered front window, then dropped low. He had to assert himself, to let the guy know they would fight to the death if they had to.

Silence.

They needed a line of sight. And he knew exactly how to get it. He glanced at Meghan. "Remember the op with the interpreter who wanted to be a stand-up comedian?"

She grinned, the sight totally out of place given their current situation. "I'll take the upstairs."

The most dangerous maneuver, requiring her to cross the open space between their meager shelter and the stairs. If she was hit doing the job he ought to be doing, he'd never be able to forgive himself.

He grabbed her arm. "I'll go."

"Because you know the layout of my house so well." She jerked her arm away and crouched low, gone before he could argue.

He followed the sounds of her creaking up the stairs. *Lord, keep her safe.*

Another bullet shattered a pane in one of the front windows and cracked into the stone above the fireplace. *Please.*

Tate was the proverbial sitting duck behind the couch. The wood and fabric wouldn't stop a bullet, and if the shooter got brave and charged the front door, there would be a shoot-out.

He massaged the grip of his gun. He had to take control of the situation and let the shooter know who was really in charge here.

Keeping low, he crept to the far corner of the room, wide-open to view should the shooter burst through the front door, but out of the immediate line of sight. Edging along the wall, he peeked between the curtain and the window, careful not to move the fabric and give himself away. He scanned the small sliver of trees he could see, looking for anything that would indicate the sniper's position. A muzzle flash. The glint of sunlight on metal. A branch moving against the wind.

He saw nothing.

Upstairs, the floor creaked, Meghan moving from the front to the rear of the house to evaluate their escape route.

Nothing moved outside, but Meghan had been right about her car. The left rear tire was completely deflated. Same for the pickup. Not incapacitated, but it would be a tough escape on flats.

Another crack resounded, and the other rear tire blew, melting into a shapeless mass.

Well, their options were easier now.

Where was their shooter? They were trapped until they spotted him, and even then, if the guy had a high-powered rifle, he could keep them pinned here forever with only Meghan's revolver and Tate's semiautomatic to protect them. Powerful enough at close range, but no match for a rifle from a distance.

Tate fought the weight of failure hardening in his gut. Answers would have to wait. They had to back away or they wouldn't live to ask the questions. Everything in him wanted to take this fight head-to-head, but wisdom dictated he live to fight another day.

Glass upstairs shattered as another gunshot cracked,

closer this time. The muzzle flash came from the left, toward the curve in the driveway, high in a tree.

He'd found the shooter.

A second shot and a thud from above sent him scrambling for the stairs.

Had Meghan been hit?

TEN

Meghan dropped hard as a bullet whacked the side of the house way too close to her position, the laptop she'd retrieved from the closet clattering to the floor. She stretched to grab the machine and crept toward the bedroom door.

From the sound of it, the shooter was definitely somewhere to the left of the house.

She hoped there wasn't more than one.

They had a chance to get out without being seen, but they had to leave now. If he moved before they reached cover, there was no way to pinpoint what his line of sight would be from a new position.

She edged down the stairs and found Tate at the bottom, on his way up. Keeping low, she slipped in next to him, back pressed against the wall out of the line of sight of the window by the door. "He's to the left."

"I saw him." Tate reached for her, running his hands along her arms. "You hit?"

Even in the midst of everything, his touch rattled her. She jerked away. "What? No." They didn't have time for this. "We need to go."

Tate tapped the barrel of his pistol. "Shooter's in a

tree to the left of the driveway, about three hundred yards out. He's blind to the left center of the backyard from there."

"How many?"

"Saw one, but there's no guarantee there aren't more. We can't give him a chance to get between us and the barn."

Meghan didn't want to sneak out. She needed the identity of the mystery man who'd overshadowed half of her life. She angled toward the kitchen. "We can go out the back and flank him. If—" She half rose, ready to roll, but Tate pulled her lower.

"I'd love to, but no. From his position, he's got a full view around himself. There's no way to stay hidden. He's got the height advantage, too." Tate shook his head. "We're not going to be stupid."

Meghan grasped her pistol harder, the grip digging into her fingers. She didn't want to listen to Tate, but she did want them both to survive.

Man, how she hated to step away from a battle. "I've got a go bag in the laundry room near the back door." She didn't wait for Tate to take the lead. It was bad enough she had to run. She wasn't going to be the tail end of the train.

Another crack, and a section of Sheetrock opposite the fireplace crumbled.

He was firing blind potshots. That was one relief, however small.

Around the corner in the kitchen, she stood and stared at the floor, a sudden wave of despair shoving her heart into her throat. She'd probably never see this place again now that it was compromised. The floors she'd worked so hard on, the dreams she'd planned so meticulously...

Tate grabbed her hand. "I know." His voice was deeper than she'd ever heard it, his touch driving home the grief she couldn't stop.

His tenderness nearly undid her. Knowing his story, there was no doubt he understood. He was probably reliving the day he'd had to flee the place he'd called home.

Meghan's long-dreamed-for life ended when she walked out the door, whether the shooter got sights on her or not. Whoever he was, he'd already taken everything. She felt like shaking her fist at the sky. *Thanks for the help.*

"I..." Tate exhaled loudly, his fingers tightening on hers. "We've got to go. You'll have to grieve later." Regret tinged his urgency.

She jerked away. *No.* There wouldn't be any grief. There was only moving forward. She'd learned to keep putting one foot in front of the other long ago. "Let's go." She stepped around him, reaching into the laundry room to grab a black backpack as she passed. She shoved it at him and pulled a broom from beside the door.

Tate caught her plan and shoved the backpack into her chest, snatching the broom as she struggled to keep the bag from slipping to the floor.

He eased her to the side, out of range of the door. "No way am I letting you in the line of fire first."

It had gone this way more than once. Yes, they'd been partners, but he had a sense of chivalry that drove him to protect her.

And she hated the way something inside her responded.

Tate eased to the window over the sink and crouched beneath cabinet level, letting the broom hover before he used the bristles to sweep the curtain aside, as though someone peeked through the sheer material.

From her position by the door, Meghan waited, tense, watching for the gunshot that would indicate the back of the house was covered.

Nothing.

Tate waited another second, then moved the curtain again.

Silence.

Meghan rocked back on her heels, unsure if she was relieved or doubly concerned. A shot would have been a definitive answer. Silence could mean anything.

Tate dropped the broom with a clatter and met her by the door, taking a knee beside her. "Ready?"

Raising on her toes to peek out the window, she nodded, her shoulder brushing Tate's chest. "Keep left across the yard. We'll cut through the trees and skirt the—"

Tate was looking at her oddly, watching her mouth as she talked. Something zipped between them, the same something she'd felt more than once on their last few missions. The same something that had driven her to run the last time.

Nothing had changed since they'd been apart. She'd mourned him for years because she loved him.

And the love hadn't died. If anything, it had flamed to life, wrapping her in a paralysis that grounded her to the floor, drove her headlong into a moment totally out of step with the danger outside the door.

Into a danger more frightening than a shot to the heart from a hidden sniper.

She inhaled slowly, balancing her thoughts. Now could not be a worse time, and she finally understood why Ethan had warned her away from Tate Walker. Emotion took the focus off the threat and placed it squarely where it shouldn't be.

Meghan reached a trembling hand out and pulled the door open, squeezing past Tate. "Let's go."

She hit the porch steps determined to leave her grief dead on the kitchen tile, every muscle tensed against the thud of a bullet into her torso.

Tate was close behind, his breaths louder than her own.

There were about a hundred yards between them and the cover of the trees. Without glancing over her shoulder, trusting Tate to guard the rear, she examined the area, practiced eyes watching for movement, then dived for the trees.

She hit cover and kept running, not stopping until she was on the other side of the thin grove of oaks dividing the pasture from the house. Even then, she kept moving, shoving through creeping underbrush at a pace restrained only enough to keep her from sprawling, the victim of an errant tree root.

"They'll figure out we're gone soon." Tate pulled in beside her, breathing heavily in the thick air. "We'll follow the edge of the wood line to the barn."

"Gotcha." Meghan leaned against a thick tree trunk to heave in air as though she'd never get enough, then pushed off and kept moving. "Trail's to the right when you get the truck out." She hefted her go bag higher on her shoulder. "They'll hear the truck rattle the minute you start it."

"Then I'll drive fast." He sounded as winded as she felt. Probably doubly so, considering what he'd lost to a would-be assassin's knife.

At the edge of the woods, Meghan dropped to one knee to survey the area. Nothing moved except branches waving in the slight breeze. The smell of fresh-cut grass drifted from the house, the lazy summer scent a counterpoint to their danger.

"It's doubtful they know the truck is here." Tate's voice was low beside her where he'd taken a position similar to hers, watching to make sure no one followed. His shoulder brushed hers.

As crazy as it felt in this uncertain chaos, she wanted to lean against him and let him hold her, to accept the support he'd always offered, to acknowledge the way he let her take the lead now so he could follow, standing between her and danger.

Always standing between her and danger.

The implication she couldn't take care of herself ought to fire her anger, but instead it made her want to surrender even more.

But she wouldn't. Ever. And now would be the craziest time to fall into the trap of needing someone else, when both of them could be in a sniper's crosshairs. "If you've got the rear, we'll go."

They slipped into the barn, the air hot and still under the roof where the breeze couldn't reach. It was heavier than a horse blanket, and the heat of the day meant it smelled twice as bad as it had earlier.

Tate coughed. "You sure the horses aren't still in here?"

"Yeah." Meghan breathed through her mouth, but it didn't help. "Tell me you have the keys."

"Still in my pocket."

A shout bounced across the pasture from the house, and another echoed.

Their friend's backup had arrived, and they'd discovered the house was empty.

In the dim light, Meghan caught Tate's eye across the roof of the truck, then she pitched her go bag into the bed and leaped for the back barn door that led to an overgrown trail and the main road.

The truck rocked as Tate jumped in, slammed the door hard, then leaned across the small space to throw her door open.

Meghan unlatched the barn door and strained against heavy wood and rusted metal rollers no one had moved in years. She threw her back against the small opening and pushed off the door frame with her feet, leveraging every ounce of her weight. The rollers caught and the door moved, slowly at first before gaining speed, flooding the barn with sunlight and fresh air.

Tate fired the engine, and Meghan jumped in as he rolled past, pulling her seat belt across with a click. "Drive the way you used to. I promise not to complain."

The truck bounced as it hit a rut at the edge of the trail; a pinging whack rang through the vehicle.

Tate's mouth drew into a grim line. "They hit us. Stay low."

Meghan ignored him, whirling in the seat to see two men enter the clearing, one bearing a sniper rifle he aimed at the truck.

Meghan slid the rear window open and raised her

gun, but the bounce of the vehicle kept her from getting a clear shot.

"Get down!" Tate yelled as another bullet thudded against the truck bed.

Instead of obeying the order, she pressed herself tight against the seat and tried to level a clear shot.

They were feet from the trees when the window behind Tate shattered.

Fire burned Tate's shoulder as glass rained into the vehicle and a bullet thudded into the top of the dash. He fought to keep the truck from bouncing in a rut, when what he really wanted was to reach for Meghan. "Are you hit?"

Meghan dived sideways, planting her back flat against the passenger door as she watched the rear. "No. You?"

Tate didn't answer, simply urged the truck on as he shifted through the gears. *Lord, let this truck run better than it ever has before.*

The vehicle, probably twenty years old, wasn't a high-performance anything. It was part of his cover as a disgruntled former soldier in need of a paycheck. He'd never expected to use it as a getaway car along a rutted horse path through the woods. What he wouldn't give for his Jeep... Or his motorcycle. Or anything other than this.

He gripped the wheel tighter, ignoring the pain in his shoulder as another bullet shattered the mirror on the driver's door.

The truck leaped forward as though it felt the pain, gaining cover in the trees.

"How far to the road?" The question came out

through gritted teeth. He doubted the truck could make it much longer without bouncing the transmission onto the overgrown dirt path.

"Not much." Meghan relaxed a little and shoved her hair out of her face. Her forehead wrinkled. "You're hit." She reached toward his shoulder, her fingers bouncing in time with the truck as it careened into ruts.

She didn't have to tell him. The curve of his shoulder throbbed with every bump in the road. He didn't dare inspect the wound but kept praying the truck survived. They didn't have time to doctor a flesh wound.

Tate's jaw ached from clenching it. "Will we beat them to the road?"

"It'll be close. There's a side road if you turn toward the house. It eventually brings you to the highway." She reached for him again. "I need to check out—"

"Let's get you to safety first." Human nature was to turn away from the threat. If Tate could make it to the side road, the shooters would streak by it, never thinking Tate would be so bold.

If they made it that far.

Ahead, the trees opened, a glimpse of wavering black pavement appearing between them.

Tate had never been so happy to see asphalt in his life. He skidded the truck to a halt, downshifting through the throbbing in his shoulder. Hanging a right, he speed-shifted as fast as the old truck would let him, barely slowing at the turn that appeared on the left. The truck rattled and protested as Tate pushed it to its ancient limits, but it complied.

Maybe he'd rethink his opinion of the metal beast.

Tate watched the road while Meghan turned to cover behind them.

About five minutes later, she settled into the seat, facing forward. "I think we made it."

Tate took his first deep breath in what felt like hours, though the whole ordeal had lasted less than fifteen minutes. His heart pounded, the immediacy of the moment waning and letting the what-ifs settle in. He shoved them away. Dealing in what might have happened kept him from focusing on what needed to happen. They'd made their getaway, and now they had to find a place to regroup. "Thank You, Lord."

Meghan turned toward him and started to say something. Instead, she holstered her sidearm, then reached over and lifted the sleeve of his T-shirt, leaning closer. Her touch was gentle, belying the usual boisterous way she attacked life. She inspected the injury, raising a whole other kind of sensation where the caress trailed, one that overrode pain, pumping through his heart and out into his entire being.

"They grazed the side of your shoulder. Probably burns like nobody's business, but it's superficial. Where's the first aid kit?"

Tate swallowed hard, riding a wave of adrenaline, dangerously close to getting sucked into a place he'd never want to leave. "What makes you sure there is one?" His voice cracked from the strain of not looking at Meghan. What he might see if he did was more terrifying than a bullet shattering his shoulder. He couldn't trust emotions born out of a near-death experience, no matter how much he wanted to.

She laughed, the sound loud in the small truck. "Walker, there's always a first aid kit. You're like the guy in the old TV show who could fix a gas leak with chewing gum and chocolate. Always prepared."

No arguing that. "It's under the seat." There was always a contingency to think about, and he made sure he covered every base, but he'd missed one. He'd never counted on feeling anything even close to this at Meghan's touch.

He tightened his focus on the road. *Think, Walker. You cannot ever pull this truck over and kiss her the way you're thinking about kissing her. Ever.* "How did they find us?" He had his suspicions, but he wanted to hear her theory first.

"Were you followed last night?" Her voice stretched as she leaned over and felt for the first aid kit.

"No." She should know better than to ask. He'd never bring danger to her, not if he could prevent it.

"Your phone?"

"It links to the team through a secure network and pings a half a dozen different satellites before it connects. It would take weeks to track." And he'd have to use it to call Ethan soon, let the team leader know he was on the run with their last known link to the hacker. "Yours?"

"Battery is out and it's in the safe at the house. Any other tech on you?"

"No."

"Then I have no idea."

"I think you do." She was smarter than that. The Meghan he'd known investigated every possibility without mercy. There was no way she was missing the biggest one of all.

"Not Phoebe." The conviction in her voice bordered on anger. "I've known her too long. The Snyder Foundation is clean. Her father's company is clean. I checked."

"You can't ignore the fact she's known you since college." Tate rotated his hands on the steering wheel, the smooth plastic warming in his palms. "She links what happened in your past to today. Does she know about your hacking? Your military experience?"

"Not about the hacking. Nobody knows about it but you. I was in ROTC, so she knows I was an officer. She thinks I was an IT specialist. There's no reason for her to believe otherwise. She's not a suspect."

"Somebody she knows might be. Follow the chain. Who else might Phoebe have told?"

"No one." The assertion held a finality Tate knew better than to argue with.

"And Yvonne?" The woman's behavior today still didn't sit right with Tate. For someone who was one of Meghan's closest confidants, the woman had been anything but friendly.

Meghan laughed, but it was a harsh, bitter sound. "She's a tech zero. She can barely check her email."

He tried to relax and not give away the tension pushing into his muscles. Meghan was too close to the situation. When he called in his suspicions to Ethan, he'd have to do it outside her hearing. "Anyone else?" They were missing something, but he couldn't pin his thoughts to what.

She ran the zipper along the canvas first aid bag, the sound grating. "My circle is small. I don't have a lot of friends."

The pain she didn't reveal in the words pulsed through him. Her circle was small because she purposely kept it small, afraid of more abandonment. And he'd pretended to be dead, leaving her even more adrift.

Tate glanced at the rearview again, the heaviness in his chest having nothing to do with exertion or adrenaline. Meghan McGuire—his partner, his friend, the woman who'd thrown his life sideways when she left— had been living in fear for years. Fear she'd never shared with him. Fear she'd carried by herself. She kept a bag packed for the day she'd have to escape and walked around forever looking behind her, unable to grasp a future where she was free.

The same way he'd done.

He released the wheel with his right hand, joints protesting the strain of the past few minutes, and laid his fingers over hers, stilling her fidgeting.

She stiffened, and Tate thought she was going to pull away, so he tightened his fingers around hers, not giving her the opportunity. "You're not alone now, Meg. If you'd told me about being blackmailed earlier, you never would have been."

She stared at their hands, then turned toward the side window, the hum of the truck tires the only sound in the cab.

The trees grew denser as they drove east, the thick woods pressing in, darkening the day and cooling the air in the cab with heavy shadows, helping the ancient air conditioner make things more comfortable. Tate had no idea where he was, not physically and not emotionally, not with Meg's hand in his and not with killers somewhere behind them. Like the day he'd nearly died, like the night a group of thugs kicked in his door and ran him out of his home, the world had changed and left him without a map.

Finally, Meghan swallowed so hard it was audible. "I didn't know what would happen." She pulled away from him and opened the bag, the zipper grating across Tate's nerves. "I still don't."

"I told you——"

"Don't." She tore the paper from a large bandage. "I hacked a university's donor database. I turned over stolen identities to a terrorist. There's no excusing the crime, no matter what I did to fix it." She pressed the bandage gently over his arm, not lingering this time. "When we stop, I'll clean it, but at least you won't leak blood on yourself for the time being."

She'd shut the door on the conversation, but Tate still had his foot in the opening, and he wasn't about to let her stop without fighting for her future. "You were blackmailed. You tried to make it right. I think your service record——"

"Was built on a lie."

Where was this all coming from? In the years they'd worked together, she'd shown no chinks in her armor, no insecurities. Not the way she did now. "You'd be fine if Phoenix hadn't come back."

"I'd be fine if you hadn't come back."

Tate winced. Well, at least he knew where he stood.

"Tate, I…I'd grieved you. I'd let you go. I'd managed to somehow forget the way I used to feel——" She stopped, then huffed through pursed lips. "It's not you—it's all of this. There's a new normal. One that might include me running for my life forever."

ELEVEN

"Hotel."

Meghan jerked away from the window and blinked twice, the world a muted wash outside her sunglasses. She shoved her fingers between the lenses and her face, scrubbing her eyes. "What time is it?"

"A little after nine." Tate pulled the sunglasses from her face, giving her a clearer view of the little hotel sprawling across a parking lot in front of them. Weeds grew around the brick building, and the siding could use a good power wash, but it certainly wasn't the worst place they'd ever taken refuge in. "We're in middle of nowhere Ohio, in case you're wondering."

Meghan pulled her neck from side to side, trying to stretch the effects of sleeping against a bouncing truck window out of her neck. "We don't have to stop. I can drive for a while."

"Probably better if we both put in some quality sleep in actual beds." He popped the door open and slid out, leaning in with laughter dancing in his green eyes. "You're cute when you snore." He flashed her a grin and was gone before her sleep-fogged mind could devise a retort.

Cute. Not a word anyone had ever applied to her before. The sentiment danced across Meghan's skin as Tate walked toward the small hotel office, the deep shadows of late evening making him look like a dream in more ways than one. He was definitely easy to watch, even more so since he carried himself with his typical confidence.

He made her want to chase him across the parking lot and dump her heart on the pavement, but acting like a teenager was decidedly out of bounds.

Even if he had called her cute.

She checked her holster, then sat watching the parking lot until Tate returned, refusing to let her mind wander to why he'd chosen the sentiment, even in a jab. She scrubbed at her cheeks. Man, she definitely needed sleep if she was going to read this much into one little word.

Tate slid into the truck and passed her a key. She held it in front of her and let the dull metal catch the glow of a streetlight. "You're kidding. They use real keys here?" Surely every hotel in the world had gone to cards by now.

"And they take cash." Tate cranked the protesting truck and drove it around to the rear of the building out of sight from the road. "We'll have to think about other transportation soon. I'll make a quick check of the area in the morning, see if I can't find a used car lot."

"Be hard to trade with the exterior sporting ventilation à la bullet."

"The right amount of money can silence even the nosiest of questions."

He was right. Another experience they'd shared many times.

Meghan patted the dashboard before she snagged the first aid kit and got out, reaching for her backpack in the truck bed. She'd miss the old clunker. It had, after all, gotten them out of a shoot-out. Seemed mean to put her out to pasture in some backwoods used car lot.

If she was nostalgic for a truck, then Tate was right. She needed real sleep. She'd already slipped about her feelings for him once, on the edge of an adrenaline high, and she didn't need to make her slip a complete fall on her face.

She followed Tate along a surprisingly clean hallway. It exuded the smell every other hotel in the world had, the scent no one could identify other than to call it "hotel smell."

Meghan let herself relax a little. At least the place didn't reek of stale food and cigarette smoke. Hopefully the bed was clean.

Not that it mattered. She'd slept on foreign dirt with camel spiders. She could take on pretty much anything at this point.

No longer trusting herself to speak, she threw a wave to Tate and shoved open the door to the room next to his, dropping her bag to the floor and herself to the edge of the bed, collapsing flat on her back before she realized she was still holding the first aid kit.

Tate's arm. It still needed real attention. Attention she'd have to give it as soon as he finished his phone conversation. Through the thin wall, she could hear his voice rising and falling, probably calling in their day to Ethan. The low rumble of him doing his job—the job they'd once shared—ran from her stomach to her heart in tiny shivers she was too tired to fight. She'd felt it all the way up her arm and into her soul earlier when he touched her hand. She was still full-fledged in love with the man who'd stolen her heart years ago.

There would never be a good time to tell him. He had a life she no longer wanted, a plan she couldn't fit into her life. She wouldn't ask him to stay any more than she'd pack her things and go run all over the world with him.

No. She'd grieved for him once and was certain she couldn't survive grieving for him again. Distance was best.

A knock dragged her straight to her feet. No way she'd fallen asleep, but the proof was in her grogginess and the fact she was still clutching the canvas first aid bag as if it were a teddy bear.

This nightmare would never end.

Another knock, softer this time, on a door she hadn't noticed before, standing between the two rooms. She tucked the kit under her arm and pulled herself taller, steeling herself against the attraction she was too tired to fight as she pulled open the door.

Tate looked as weary as she felt. He'd had a shower while she slept, and now he smelled like soap and shampoo, his hair damp and towel tousled. But something in his expression wasn't lit the way it usually was.

"Everything okay?"

He seemed to come back from somewhere else. "Yeah. I just…" He pointed at the first aid kit. "Arm's killing me, and you're holding the painkillers."

Without caring about consequences, she lifted his shirtsleeve to check the bandage she'd slapped into place earlier. Blood seeped through. "It might need a couple of stitches."

He grimaced and stepped into the room, sinking into

a chair by the small wooden table. "Make it quick. I need sleep." He'd hit the proverbial wall. It wasn't hard to miss the change in attitude.

She saluted and dug through the bag, confident in her abilities, if not in her emotions. "Cranky when you're in pain, aren't you?"

"Nope. I've been on the other end of your needle before. You sew crooked stitches. I want pretty scars."

Meghan rolled her eyes, swallowing a retort. She was crashing fast, and her filter was crumbling even faster. The less she said and the less she touched him, the better. Careful to keep her touch off his skin as much as possible, she peeled away the bandage for a closer inspection.

It definitely qualified as a graze, which meant even less touching. "Well, you don't have to worry about my needle skills." She made quick work of cleaning the wound, ignoring him when he winced, and had a proper bandage in place before she could think twice about lingering. "All done. You can sleep now." It was abrupt, but she knew her limits. Much longer in the same space and she'd kick apart every wall inside just to have Tate Walker's arms around her.

"Wow." Tate stood and walked to the door between their rooms. "You have a good evening, too."

She followed, wanting him to leave and wanting to follow him when he did. "I'm tired, and you know what happens when we both get tired."

"We fight like an old married couple." Maybe the sentiment was supposed to be funny, but it sounded tender, an unexpected brush on Meghan's heart.

Tears pricked the back of her nose, further evidence she was skating the edge.

Tate didn't make a move to shut the door. Instead, he swiped an errant tear from her cheek, his touch fiery. "Why did you leave?" The rough edges of his voice strummed across her heart.

She wanted to lean into him, to give in and quit fighting. She backed off. "Partners shouldn't work together too long. They get too close." Meghan stepped sideways to skirt Tate, but he grabbed her bicep.

"What do you mean by 'too close'?" His voice was husky, and he watched her, looking for something she couldn't begin to calculate.

Those words may have been the worst she'd ever chosen. Meghan pulled, but his grasp tightened. He wouldn't let her go until she gave him an answer.

It had better be a good one, or they'd stand here forever while the bad guys drew closer. Meghan swallowed hard, determined not to be the first to back down, even though he had a wonder about him, as though he was seeing something he'd never seen before. Her blood pressure drove into orbit as heat washed across her skin and stole readiness from her muscles.

She wouldn't retreat, but he was welcome to back away anytime.

He didn't. Tate pulled her closer, until his warmth filtered through her shirt. His eyes dropped to her lips before sliding to hers again. "What's 'too close,' Meg?"

"This." The word came out in a harsh whisper, forced to squeeze past the lump lodged in her throat.

Here it was, right in front of her. The whole reason she'd bucked the army and left him in the first place. The undeniable reality that this man simply standing beside her would never be enough, that his touch on her arm wasn't what she wanted.

She didn't want a partner. She wanted Tate Walker to love her. To look at her exactly the way he was looking at her right now, with an incomprehensible expression she'd never seen before but had always believed would feel exactly this way.

Noting else mattered. Not the fact that an assassin had them in the crosshairs. Not the fact that there was a mission demanding their attention. Not the fact that a hacker had his finger poised over a panic button they had yet to identify.

The outside world meant nothing in this space between them. The space rapidly shrinking as Tate leaned closer and drew her toward him at the same time.

He swallowed hard, his breath tightening, too close. His searching never wavered.

Meghan moved to push him away, but her palm landed on his chest, right over this heart; the pace of his matched the pace of her own. Too fast, the rhythm drawing her in.

He slipped his arm around her waist, closing the distance between them, letting his hand on her bicep slide to her neck, where his thumb brushed her pulse. He pressed a kiss to her forehead and stayed there, not moving, letting something pass between them that defied words but pulsed against her heart like a whole new way of living.

Meghan let go of the tension she'd been holding for years, balling her fists into his shirt, her toes curling into her shoes. She tilted her head, breaking his touch against her forehead, but only long enough to meet again, her lips brushing his once before he kissed her without hesitation, without reserve, kicking through the walls she'd built between them for years.

In one moment, she lost herself, her past, her fears...
and this man was all that mattered.

Tate Walker was a goner.

He was a planner. A thinker. A man who found the
best of himself working from the inside out.

Kissing Meghan McGuire was a body blow that
slammed him from the outside in. There had always
been something about her, but he'd never dreamed her
something was the missing piece meant to fill every
remaining empty place inside.

When mist had covered her eyes, Tate had cracked,
every feeling he'd never admitted to himself seeping
through. Meghan overtook his well-disciplined rationality.

He'd needed to know why she'd left him, and the
shades of truth behind her answer had completely un-
done him. The cracks blew open like a dam breaking,
and he was swept away in the current.

She was dangerous, stealing the control he'd always
prided himself on. Taking away the authority he'd always maintained. Challenging him the way no one else
ever could.

His emotions swirled and threatened to pull him
under until he had to break the kiss or risk drowning
in her. He slid his lips from hers, lingering in the tender
place beside her mouth, then pulled her closer, resting
his chin on her hair, never wanting to walk away from
this moment. They could stay here like this, in the saf-
est place he'd ever been. In the one place where he'd
ever felt as though he actually belonged.

In a sharp rush that nearly ran him over, he knew.
The restlessness he'd been fighting, the moments he'd

felt off sync with her. It wasn't because they'd grown apart; it was because he wanted them to grow closer. He was in love with this woman who released her death grip on his shirt to slip her arms around his waist so she could stand with him in a way he'd never imagined she would. He closed his eyes, blocking out everything else.

This. This was home.

What just happened was about to change every game they'd ever played in. Boy, did they need to talk. A lot.

Meghan didn't seem any more inclined to pull away than he did, so he held her close, planted a kiss to the top of her head and gave them both the time to deal with whatever this was, with all the answers falling into place. Answers to questions she might have had all along, but he was just beginning to form.

Questions she might have had all along...

Suddenly it all made sense. The way she'd pulled away in those last few months on the job, had changed the way she talked to him, had limited the amount of time she'd spent with him outside work. "You left the army because of me."

Her body went rigid in his arms; then she pushed away, gaze planted firmly on his chest. "We both need sleep. We're letting ourselves get—"

"If you say something as cliché as 'that never should have happened,' I promise you, Meg, I'll..." *Kiss you again.* He shoved his fists into his pockets to keep from reaching for her.

Maybe she was right. Maybe exhaustion was dogging them both and wrecking their judgment. Or maybe exhaustion was battering walls that never should have been built in the first place. All he knew was, it might be a cliché all on its own, but he was definitely colder without her in his arms.

But he didn't reach for her. He knew better.

Meghan opened the distance between them, raising her face to his. She was no more ready to end this than he was; it was clear by the way she looked at him. "We're both out of the reserves it's going to take to use our heads right now."

He puffed out a breath. She was right, and he should have thought of it first. It was his job to protect her not only from people who wanted her dead but from himself, as well.

Still, no part of him wanted to put the brakes on what was happening. He wanted to drag her to the truck and get her far away from danger. To find a preacher and… marry her?

Oh, yeah. She was right. Reason was a goner.

Reason said this was a road they needed to stay far away from. He'd walked it once before, and the fact he'd become a believer and Stephanie hadn't had wrecked their marriage.

As much as he wanted to push everything else aside and kiss Meghan again, this had to stop here. Her ideas about God were muddled at best, and flat wrong at worst, and he couldn't risk wrecking the two of them, no matter how much he knew he was falling in love with her.

He balled his hands into tight fists. For her, he'd throw experience away and risk everything, but he couldn't. When he lost her—

His phone vibrated in his pocket, the device pulsing the staccato rhythm identifying Ethan on the other end.

He couldn't ignore the team leader, not now, no matter how much he wanted to.

Meghan had backed into her room and was watching him with concern, as if she could see his internal struggle playing out on his face. She pointed toward his phone with a tight smile. "I can hear your phone buzzing. Answer it. I'm going to grab a shower and then try to sleep." She pulled farther away, then stopped, a small smile teasing the corners of her mouth, making Tate want to forget all reason and dive in for another kiss. And another. "Go ask the manager if you can vacuum the lobby. It's almost like mowing grass." She gave him one more long look and shut the door between them.

Nothing in his life had ever seemed so final.

Pulling the phone from his pocket gave him something to do other than beating through the wood to tell her common sense didn't matter.

Tate pulled the phone to his ear. "Yeah?" With the uneven tone in his voice, Ethan was bound to know something was up.

But the other man was all business. "We need to talk."

"Give me a second." He snapped the demand as if it were a dry twig, not ready for Ethan to pile more onto him. He needed time to think, to clear his mind. He'd finally realized he loved Meghan McGuire. He'd held her in his arms.

And he couldn't have her.

He wanted to put his fist through the wall. Never in his life had he wanted anything as much as he wanted to throw himself all in to life with her, even though it was ill advised. Never.

He cast one more look at the door between them, the tug toward her almost too much to bear.

He'd been right before. She was dangerous.

"Let me know when you're clear." Something in Ethan's voice reached through the phone and slapped Tate to sensibility. There was a mission boiling hot, and they were smack in the center of the fire. He could never forget the urgency again, not if he wanted to get Meghan out of this alive with her reputation intact.

All exhaustion and emotion fled. He paced to the window in the corner farthest from the wall adjoining Meghan's room. "Talk."

Ethan exhaled heavily. He'd been on this mission a whole lot longer than Tate had. Tracking Phoenix had taken a toll on them all, and the entire team was ready to end this and stop the murder and the madness. "You guys made the local news, and it's not good. I've sent you a link."

That wasn't the worst thing that could have happened. It was coming, expected even. "We can deal with—"

"That's not all. The program, the one Meghan sent to Ashley this afternoon. What did she tell you about it?"

This was about Meghan's software? Pride for the work Meghan had done with him and the work she'd done since she left him swelled. He may have to bury what he felt for her, but that didn't mean he could kill the feelings. "She wrote it. She's been working on it since she got out. Her plan was—"

"Tate."

Gravity dragged Tate's respect for Meghan to the ground with a thud.

"Did anyone else work on it with her?"

"I doubt it. She's the same loner she's always been." Tate gripped the phone tighter. "What are you not saying?"

There was a long silence, so long it left Tate holding his breath until he saw spots dancing in his vision. When Ethan spoke, he sounded as though he'd rather be saying anything else. "Ashley was digging through the code, pretty impressed with what Meghan put together. It's a tight program. It's an untraceable tracker. The software can pinpoint a user to the way they dot their i's." The words were flattering, but the tone? The tone was entirely different.

"Stop beating around the bush."

"It started to feel like déjà vu to her, so Ashley started digging. The program—line for line—was used in the hack on Staff Sergeant Jessica Dylan's machine in Kentucky."

Tate sagged against the wall, his injured shoulder protesting the pressure. Phoenix had followed their every move then, had aided and abetted a terrorist who was killing soldiers in order to steal their identities. They had been in Kentucky when they'd realized they were pitted against a hacker who scared even them.

It was possible Tate might be sick, right here. He might not be as tech savvy as Meghan or Ashley or even Ethan, but he knew it was impossible for two separate people to write line-for-line identical code. Monkeys were more likely to type Shakespeare.

"Tate."

"Don't say it." Every dream he'd ever had, every desire he'd let loose standing in Meghan's room and holding her in his arms crashed into a million pieces at his feet.

"Ashley, Sean and I have all hit at it from every angle." Ethan charged on as though Tate had never said a word. "There's no way around it. You have to find out if Meghan McGuire is working with Phoenix."

TWELVE

Tate drew back his arm, ready to throw his phone against the wall and watch it smash into pieces, but then he dropped his arm, his hold on the device so tight his entire arm ached.

There was no way Meghan was the enemy. Ethan had to know that. He knew Meghan almost as well as Tate did. Although Tate was fairly certain his team leader had never shared a kiss with her.

Feeling for all the world as if somebody had sucker punched him in the gut, he let the phone clatter to the floor. Dropping to the edge of the bed, Tate gripped his head in his hands, wishing he'd skipped the burger from a drive-through a couple of hours ago.

Their kiss never should have happened. His emotions never should have happened. But they had, and now they filmed his judgment, a hurricane between his heart and mind. The clear thinking he'd always prided himself on got lost in the mess, making it hard to study the evidence objectively, to grasp onto what might be true…and what might be false.

Scooping up his phone, he shoved it into his pocket and stalked for the door between their rooms, stopping at the entrance. He could charge in there demanding answers, but it would get him nowhere. She'd continue with the lie if she was guilty.

She'd hate him if she wasn't.

In his whole life, Tate had never felt so helpless and out of control, not even when Stephanie took off. When it came to this case, everywhere he turned was a mistake, everything went from bad to worse. When he cleaned up one mess, a worse one surfaced. He felt as though God had taken him to the end of himself and left him there, reminding him there was nowhere else to turn but up.

Lord, tell me what to do.

A soft sound from the hallway brought a halt to the prayer.

Slipping to the door, Tate stood to the side, back to the wall, focusing everything on the slight shuffle filtering through the thin wood.

The shuffle that came from next door.

Here was the whole problem with the past half hour. He'd let Meghan get to him the way no woman ever had before. She'd managed to steal his edge, made him forget they were being pursued and the stakes were too high to drop his guard. Now someone lurked outside. It could be a maid working late or another hit man sent their way.

Only one way to find out.

Steeling himself for whatever might come next, Tate turned the knob and threw the door open.

A man jumped away from Meghan's door, eyes wide, startled by the sudden movement. He was about Tate's height and had all the marks of one of those guys who loved upper-body strength and forgot to do leg work. The cocky gym-rat type who was always arrogant enough to think they could win because they'd watched a little MMA on TV.

And their arrogance made them somewhat predictable.

Tate edged into the hallway, watching the other man's body language, sizing him up, not quite ready to make the first move. He balled his fists, ready for whatever came, still not able to believe he was about to go into a fistfight for the second time in two days.

If this went Tate's way, the other man would run when Tate didn't retreat. Unfortunately, there was about a fifty-fifty chance of this ending well, because the guy appeared to be muscle-for-hire, the same way Isaac and his crew had been.

Which meant Phoenix was still outsourcing his brawn, and Muscles here might be foolish enough to try anything.

The guy telegraphed his first punch, edging his shoulder back and shifting his sights to Tate's jaw before he launched his fist.

Shifting his weight to the side, Tate threw out an arm and blocked the punch, then launched his weight forward, using his attacker's momentum to force the man past him and farther down the hallway.

With a thud that shook the thin wall, his opponent cracked his shoulder into the Sheetrock and stumbled, not quite falling. Instead of turning and coming at Tate, he took off running, headed for the stairs.

Tate glanced at Meghan's door, hesitating half a second about leaving her alone before taking pursuit, bursting through the heavy door into the stairwell.

His assailant's feet pounded the stairs, and the down-stairs door burst open.

Tate couldn't let this guy get away. They were rapidly running out of options. Even though this was probably another Isaac who knew little about the inner workings of Phoenix's organization, Tate would take anything at this moment, even the number to yet another burner phone. Anything to clear Meghan and to keep her alive one more day.

The door was still swinging shut when Tate hit it, catching a glimpse of blue jeans and navy blue T-shirt rounding the corner of the building.

Tate pushed on, his chest heaving, the ache deeper than he could ever remember it being. He caught the guy around the corner and with one last burst dived into his lower back, driving him into the ground with Tate's weight added to the fall.

They hit the ground hard, Tate's blow cushioned by the bigger man's. He scrambled up enough to dig his knee into the other man's back, pressing his face into the ground with all the weight he could muster. He leaned low. "Who are you working for?" His voice carried all the anger rushing in with the adrenaline ebb. Whoever this guy was, he'd gone after Meghan. Tate ground his back teeth together, trying hard not to rear back and beat the guy into submission with ten years' worth of pent-up emotions.

"Not telling you." The dark-haired wannabe bucked, trying to throw Tate off, but Tate had the advantage.

"I think you will, or you're going to have bigger things to worry about than getting beat by somebody smaller than you." He ground his knee into spine harder, eliciting a groan. "You were doing what, just now?"

"Being neighborly."

Tate could feel his blood pressure spiking. He needed answers. Needed to know what it was going to take to save Meghan, because if he didn't do something, the hits would keep coming and, one of these times, he wouldn't be able to stop it. "You've got—"

Tires squealed and a car screamed into the rear parking lot near their position, the driver's window lowered.

Tate exhaled, suddenly even more aware of the labor in his own breathing. This was not going to end well. He'd been on the weak end of this scenario before, more than once. He was about to lose this round or die trying to win it. With his pistol in the hotel room, he had no choice but to walk away.

And the thought made him nauseous with anger and frustration.

As soon as the car ground to a halt, the shadowy form of the driver came into view, his pistol aimed straight at Tate.

Jumping backward and onto his feet, Tate edged for the corner of the building as the punk he'd had pinned to the ground jumped and ran for the car, blocking the driver's clear shot.

Tate edged around the corner out of range, then ran for the front door as the tires squealed around the back. He had to get to Meghan and get her out of here now, before those two decided to play cowboy and comb the building, if it wasn't too late already.

Meghan fluffed her damp hair, ruffling the ends and trying to make it at least somewhat presentable. If she'd been a girlier girl, she'd have thought to stash mousse or gel in her go bag along with the essentials like clothes, cash and ammo.

And she'd have packed pajamas.

She flicked her bangs one last time, then shoved her things into her backpack, slipping her holster over her belt reflexively. Having it near made her feel less helpless.

Dropping to the edge of the bed, Meghan stared at the wall, exhausted and fully convinced climbing into bed in her jeans and a T-shirt wouldn't be a bad idea as long as sleep came along. She couldn't remember the last time she'd been so desperate to shut her eyes.

But she knew sleep wasn't going to come yet, not while she had no idea what to do with their kiss. She could still feel him, the sensation of true safety, the sense of belonging he'd brought her... Meghan had had a taste of what she'd once dreamed of, and it was more than she'd expected it to be. It was a completeness she hadn't realized she was lacking. It had also done nothing to cool the fires Tate had kindled years ago, relit with his reappearance and now fanned into flame.

She loved him. Loved him with the kind of settled joy that was more right than she'd ever imagined.

It had all fallen apart when he'd pulled away from her, looking as if he was a man shocked by what he'd done, regretting it from the moment he broke their kiss.

Tate had seemed almost relieved when his phone pulled him away. Almost.

Meghan was nowhere near relieved. She was restless and antsy, torn between the urgency of their flight and the Tilt-A-Whirl of Tate's kiss. It had solidified her feelings for him, and they scared her more than anything, because if he left her the way everyone else had, where would her security lie?

With God.

Meghan paced to the window but didn't pull back the curtain. All her life she'd been cast aside. As a child, she'd scrambled for love, tried to be good enough, tried to please her mother while the woman did nothing but ignore her. Her early years didn't qualify as a childhood, more a small child taking care of her mother. No toys or stuffed animals, no family vacations or movie nights. When her mother had finally vanished for good, she'd locked away her heart, had become a terror in foster home after foster home. All she needed was herself, right?

Until, in college, she'd betrayed herself. She couldn't even trust who she thought she was.

How many times had Yvonne sat in the staff room with her and said God never changed? That He wasn't the great clock maker who backed away to watch the hands spin wildly? That He cared about Meghan and had proven it if she'd simply pay attention?

He'd proven it. Meghan had always had a place to land. Had been able to use the worst parts of herself for good in the army. Had lost Tate…but found him. Had her deepest unspoken prayers answered not only when Tate reappeared alive but every single time they'd come out of a past mission unscathed.

Life was hard, but God was always there. Standing here now, with the walls around her heart shattered by Tate's kiss, Meghan could finally see why Tate and Yvonne believed so strongly, why they knew God had been beside them during the darkest times.

The realization cracked like lightning. Meghan didn't

need Tate. She needed what Tate had. The peace that let him deal with life not by hanging on by a thread but by being held by the Creator.

She leaned back and slid down the textured wallpaper, burying her face in her knees. She was unsure what to say, unsure how to say it. All Meghan knew was she had to say something.

The room grew still, the air heavy like a warm blanket, her throat so tight she couldn't even speak out loud, but her heart…her heart knew all the right words. *God, You're real. No doubt. And You've never left me alone, even when it felt like it was just me and my wits. I need You more than I need anything, because I can't take care of myself, have never been able to.* She swiped at a tear as it broke free. *I give up. You're in charge.*

The same peace and freedom she'd felt in Tate's arms crept in, easing the tension in her muscles, radiating warmth from the inside out. Once again, there it was. Rest. Peace. Home. Not in a place, but with a person. The Person.

As much as she'd been afraid to let Tate and God in, this was the absence of fear. Tate was right.

She was finally right.

Somehow they'd find a way to be right together.

A pounding on the door between their rooms shot her to her feet, surging adrenaline that stiffened her spine even though it missed her spirit.

Meghan yanked the door open, and he charged in, brushing past her as though they'd never made a connection with each other before. Grabbing her elbow, he jerked her close, then took the gun from her holster and released her, stalking into his room, where he

dumped the bullets and pocketed them before checking the cylinder.

"What are you doing?" Meghan felt her eyes widen
as she followed him, stopping in the doorway. He'd disarmed her, and she'd let him. Surely she was asleep, and
this was a dream. "Have you lost your mind?"

He stood in the center of the room, ramrod straight,
thunderclouds blowing across his face. "Get your stuff.
We have to go."

Weariness dragged her shoulders lower. *No.* Not
when she was feet from a blanket and real sleep. "What
is going on?"

"Get your stuff. Get in the truck. Now." Tate snatched
his duffel bag and turned her shoulder toward the door.
"We'll talk in the truck."

Meghan eased into her room, half-afraid to make
any sudden moves with Tate following close behind
her. She'd never questioned his sanity before, but with
him taking her gun and stalking her like a lion, calling
Ethan to check might be a good idea.

Tate ignored her, crossing to stand by the door,
blocking the exit.

Was he afraid she was going to run? Meghan was
out of words, with no way to explain what was going
on and no way to ask. The peace she'd felt a moment
ago drifted away with Tate's agitation. Her news could
come later. Something bigger was going on.

In the truck, Tate waited until she'd fastened her seat
belt, then passed her his phone, backing out of the parking space as a news report loaded on the small device.

Her face was on the screen. Meghan's stomach curled
in on itself as she punched buttons until the announcer's

voice was clear. "…involved in an attempt to steal personal data from the school."

Yvonne appeared, talking to several police officers in the school parking lot. The announcer continued. "The school received an alert from their technical support company, warning them of an attempted data breach. McGuire, who has been the school's technical director for four years, was last seen in the company of a known gang member from Saginaw. The pair is—"

Meghan punched the lock button and stared at the blank screen, empty, the reputation she'd cultivated, the life she'd meticulously built, shattered by a hacker's lies. "I'm their technical support. There was no alert." *Unless Yvonne is lying. All of this makes less than zero sense.*

Unless Yvonne was in on it.

"What have you done?" Tate's voice was low, the kind of menacing she'd heard when he was in the midst of an interrogation with the hardest of the bad guys they'd tracked over the years.

Meghan looked up. Was he talking to her? "What?"

"What's the truth, Meghan? The whole truth?" He pointed at the phone, his arm an unwavering line ending in a point of accusation. "What have you done?" He ground out the question like gravel. "What's the whole truth?"

A whole new kind of fire blew through Meghan, anger so hot she half feared her skin might melt. She turned in the seat and went toe-to-toe with the man she knew she loved, but the man who had clearly lost his foolish mind. "It sounds a whole lot as if you're accusing me of something. And if you are, you'd better have one very, very good reason for it."

Tate dropped his arm, scanning her face; then he

turned to watch the road, a deep anguish written in the lines carved around his eyes, the circles dark underneath.

Meghan's wrath died. "Tell me what's going on."

"The team's located evidence to indicate…" The streetlights played across his face, shadows deepening and retreating. "That you're a traitor."

"Traitor?" The word hammered into Meghan's chest in a blow that drove her backward. "*Traitor* holds a seriously heavy accusation. Where is this coming from?"

"Where did you get the program you sent Ashley? The one you planted on the school's computer to track Phoenix?"

"I wrote it."

"No one worked with you?"

"No one."

Tate's face fell, the harsh lines of his countenance collapsing into something a lot less like anger and a lot more like despair. "Help me out here, Meg. Give me something…anything to say you're not involved in this."

Oh, he'd crossed a line. A great big line. "For starters, you know me, and I'd never—"

"I never thought you'd be an identity thief, either."

He might as well have thrown knives. If she tipped her chin, she was pretty sure she'd see blood pouring out of her chest. "Yesterday you said the past was forgivable." He didn't get to do this, to kiss her and make her love him, then turn on her. She leaned as close as the seat belt would let her, regaining the ground she'd given him. "Who called you, and what did they tell you?"

For a moment, he acted as though he wasn't going to speak. He'd merged onto the highway headed east before he said anything. "Ethan. Your program is the exact same one Phoenix used to trace us in Kentucky."

Meghan felt the blood drain from her face and pool in her stomach, rocking her equilibrium. "No." *Come on, God. You weren't supposed to test the trust issue this fast.* If she lost Tate, she really did have nowhere else to go but God.

"Tell me it's not you."

"How could it be me?" She touched his arm, trying to force him to look at her. He had to see she wasn't the enemy. "Why would I find out you're alive and then risk your life by having someone fire potshots at you?" She held his phone between them. "Nothing they're saying is me. The program… I wrote it. Alone. I can't explain it, but…" She wasn't making her case well. The more she talked, the more it sounded as if she were guilty. "It wasn't me." Slumping into the seat, Meghan stared out the front window, the world spinning around her.

"You don't know how badly I want to believe you." He dug his fingers into the back of his neck. "We were compromised at the hotel."

It took Meghan a second to shift gears with the change of subject. "Where are we going?"

He pulled his attention from the road long enough to read her face, then turned away. "Ethan's sending a helicopter."

For a split second, Meghan considered bailing out of the truck the next time it slowed, but running would make her appear guiltier.

But it couldn't make things worse. Tate was turning her over to his team, her former team…the team who now believed she was a terrorist.

THIRTEEN

Tate paced the small dining room at the safe house the team was currently using as a headquarters and stopped at the window. Outside, the small lawn ended abruptly in a stand of trees, the river peeking through their branches, the serenity of the scene a stark contrast to the tension indoors.

With the unit still ferreting out Craig Mitchum's treachery, their headquarters building wasn't considered fully operational, so Ethan had moved a skeleton office to a small house in the woods near the Shenandoah River.

Bracing his hands on either side of the window, Tate stared out at the green and blue of a northern Virginia summer. What he wouldn't give to be outside now, hiking off his frustrations.

But he wasn't about to leave Meghan to face his team's accusations alone, not when his heart and soul said she was innocent.

And not when he could be close by to fight for her if she needed him.

Fight for her. He sure had failed at that one. The short helicopter flight to Virginia had been a crackle of tense silence. Meghan had refused to speak to anyone once Ethan arrived to take her into custody.

Tate had had no desire to speak to anyone on his team, no longer sure what was true or who to trust. Either his team had missed the trail or Meghan had.

He was their secret weapon. The one who came in and solved the difficult problems. And this one had him stumped. Who was he if he couldn't save his team or his partner? If he couldn't protect the woman he'd fallen in love with?

His heart wanted to believe Meghan, but he'd seen too many people lie. The whole team had trusted Craig Mitchum, and it still burned how the man had betrayed and nearly killed them all. Meghan had trusted Yvonne Craft, and now the woman was smearing her name all over the press. Tate itched to investigate the principal, to see if she was part of the problem…or if she was telling the truth.

The battle tore at his insides. If Meghan was guilty, it would destroy him and—far worse than when Stephanie left—it would tilt the entire world as he knew it. *God, help me.* He needed wisdom now the way he'd never needed it before. He'd worked alongside Meghan, watched her wear herself into exhaustion on mission after mission fighting for her country. He knew her hopes and her dreams, her heart and her mind. While she'd kept her past shielded, she had never once lied to him.

Despite what Ethan Kincaid or anyone else on the team thought, Meghan was no terrorist.

As much as the evidence pointed differently, he knew Meghan was the victim here. Although if she ever heard him use such a word in her direction, she'd probably clock him again, harder than the last time.

He dropped his forehead to the glass and stared at the river glistening between the trees, the ache of doubt replaced by a raging pulse of shame. He should have gone with his instincts. He should never have let Ethan take the reins. He should have grabbed Meghan and run.

Which would have made them both fugitives.

He balled his fists and pressed them into the wall. He'd failed. *Lord, make her forgive me. Make her see I had no choice. And help me figure out what's real and what's not. Please.* Tate had to save Meghan, because nobody else could.

He shoved off the wall to go find where Ethan was questioning her. He'd march in and...

Do what? Challenge his own team? Argue she was innocent based on the fact he loved her? He balled his fists and stared at the door, more helpless than he'd ever been. He literally had no fight.

The doorknob twisted and Ethan stepped in, shutting the door behind him and standing on the other side of the scratched dining room table that served as a meeting place, feet apart and arms crossed over his chest. His dark eyes were grim and he looked more tired than Tate felt.

For the first time since Ethan had told him he was coming to bring Meghan in, Tate felt sympathy for the other man. "You hate this as much as I do."

"You know I do, Walker. She's one of us." Ethan pulled out a chair and dropped into it, the stress of their mission making him seem ten years older than the last time Tate saw him. "We have to check every angle, though, and with Phoenix, we can't take a chance."

"It could have been handled differently. There didn't have to be the drama of a helicopter in the middle of the night. You could have let me bring her in."

"You'd been compromised. Someone found you and tried to take her already." The ghost of a smile flickered on Ethan's face. "And you wouldn't have brought her in." He held up a hand to stave off the coming protest, amusement flickering out. "You wouldn't have done it any more than I'd have brought in Ashley. I did all I could to protect her when Sam Mina came after her, and that included making myself scarce when I knew orders were coming to do otherwise. Don't think I don't know you told Sean Turner to ditch his phone when the colonel was about to order him to stand down and let someone else rescue Jessica Dylan, either. No, Tate." Ethan shook his head. "You'd have vanished with her first. I'm half surprised you didn't."

"I couldn't protect her in the wild." Tate dragged a chair out and sank into it, planting his elbows on his knees. He couldn't protect her in custody, either. "What now?"

"She's insisting she's innocent and that she never gave the program to anyone and never used it until yesterday. Ashley's combing Meghan's laptop now, searching for evidence to clear her."

"I should be the one clearing her."

"You're not her savior, Tate."

"Pretty sure I'm the only one she's got." And he'd abandoned her.

"You're kidding me, Walker." Ethan laughed, the sound out of place in the whole situation.

Tate had the urge to pinch himself to make sure he

wasn't dreaming. "Right now wouldn't be the time for me to make jokes."

"And it's also not the time to lose your faith." Ethan sat forward, bracing his forearms on the scuffed table. "You're the rock to this team, always the one with the wise answers and the rock-solid plan. You know who Meghan's savior is, and you know it's not you." He sat back, crossing his arms. "Only time a guy gets this kind of God complex is when he's protecting the woman he loves and he forgets to let her go so God can do His job."

Tate could feel his hackles rising. He knew his job. And he knew His God. Who was Ethan Kincaid to—

"Tate, you know I love you, man, but you've always had one big problem. You're cocky. Somewhere along the line, you started to think you had all the answers. Now might be the time to figure out you don't." Ethan rapped his knuckles on the table and stood, all traces of amusement gone. "You'd better give Meghan to God and leave her there. And you'd better let Ashley do her job. We're doing all we can to prove Meghan's innocence. This is one time you might have to sit on the sidelines because you can't be the one to come in with guns blazing to make everything right."

Meghan propped her elbow on the arm of the small wooden chair and dropped her forehead against her palm, staring at the deep blue carpet of the bedroom Ethan was using as an office. At least they hadn't locked her in some makeshift interrogation room. Somebody here still believed in professional courtesy, not that it mattered. She hadn't missed the fact there wasn't a single piece of tech in the room. Trust only went so far.

Kneading her temples, Meghan closed her eyes

against the room's light. She had a headache that
pounded with jackhammer intensity. High winds had
made for a rough landing, a sensation that still lingered
and fought with her tension. What she wouldn't give
for an aspirin or two.

Painkillers wouldn't help her heart, though.

The whole flight to headquarters, she'd kept silent,
alternating between raging anger and shocked grief.
Tate ought to know better than to ask her those questions, and he ought to know better than to think she
could ever do something so heinous. He never should
have called in the cavalry. He should have believed in
her.

She laid her hand flat across her eyes. Problem was,
in his shoes, Meghan would probably have asked the
same questions.

The bigger problem was, even her truthful answers
made her appear guilty. Every time she'd answered
Ethan's questions, the implications of her guilt grew.
She'd written the program alone, kept the laptop secured and never uploaded the data anywhere until yesterday. If she wasn't in her own shoes, she'd wonder
about herself, too.

All of this could only mean she'd been set up. But
who would hate her enough to want to destroy her this
way?

She smirked. The list was long. As many enemies
as she and Tate had made over the course of their work
together, it could be impossible to track the truth.

The door to the room eased open, and someone drew
the chair beside her closer, but she didn't open her eyes.
Really, what new could she say? She could keep main-

taining her innocence, but until evidence proved otherwise, it wouldn't do any good.

"Meg."

She stiffened. She was either immensely relieved to hear Tate's voice or furiously angry he'd abandoned her in the first place. "What do you want?" She mumbled the question, refusing to look at him, fully aware she was acting like the worst version of her two-year-old self.

"I'm sorry."

An apology was the last thing she'd expected. Meghan turned away and rolled her eyes to the ceiling, the tears now pricking her throat. She hadn't cried since Ethan had called to tell her Tate was dead. Now she'd been fighting tears ever since he stepped into her life. It shouldn't be that way.

His sigh was loud. "I know it's not an excuse and I should have warned you, but neither Ethan nor I had a choice. The colonel told him to bring you in. Ethan gave me the chance to question you first, but with Phoenix's latest round of thugs surprising us, there was no way to ease into it." He leaned in, but he didn't touch her. "I'm sorry I couldn't stop it from happening."

More than she wanted to stay angry at him, she wanted him to close the space between them, to tell her he believed in her and he'd get her out of this.

But the job fell to someone higher than either one of them, the same someone she'd been petitioning since Ethan Kincaid wordlessly grabbed her bicep and led her onto a helicopter in the most humiliating moment of her life. At least he hadn't handcuffed her.

"No, it's not your job." Meghan pushed out of the chair and walked around the small desk to stare at a picture she'd studied from a distance all morning. It was the sole decoration in the room. Taken shortly before Meghan left the unit, after a successful mission on the other side of the world, the shot captured a moment in the life of their small military family: Meghan and Tate, Ethan and Jacob, covered in several layers of sweat and desert sand but laughing.

Ethan seemed as if his joy was incomplete, his eyes not quite matching his smile. Meghan ran a finger along the photo, stopping to grieve Jacob, then looked to Ethan's image. "He's...different now."

"He's not haunted by his choices anymore." Tate's voice was close at her shoulder. She hadn't even realized he'd gotten out of his chair. "He loved Ashley, but he left her thinking he was doing what was best for her. It was killing both of them. He was busy playing God and thinking he knew what was best..." His voice trailed off, as though he was thinking of something else. He reached over her shoulder to tap the left side of the picture, where her own face smiled. "You and Ethan look like you've got the same dog hounding you."

"Maybe I was guilty of the same thing." She turned to face him for the first time since he walked in the room. It was a couple of days after the photo when she'd confided in Ethan and he'd laid out the dangers inherent in letting emotions run free.

"Falling in love with your partner?" His voice was husky in the quiet of the office, his question loaded, but he didn't reach for her.

She looked to the side, unable to handle the way his voice fluttered inside her, skittering across her stomach and into her chest, taking the desires she'd buried for so long and magnifying them into something so strong it almost physically hurt. If he kept this up, she'd cave and tell him everything, would speak truths she could never unspeak. She'd sink into the kiss she could hear in the way he breathed, could sense easing in his posture. She could lose herself to Tate Walker and forget pain ever existed.

"You should have told me." Tate curled his finger under her chin and lifted her face, his eyes skimming her lips before rising to lock in on hers. "There was—"

A knock on the door forced them apart, and Meghan's skin grew cold. She couldn't afford to forget where she was and why she was here. Until this was over, she couldn't offer Tate anything except an uncertain future.

A woman wearing jeans and a sweatshirt, her wavy dark hair flowing to her shoulders, stepped into the room holding Meghan's laptop.

She glanced between the two of them and hesitated, as though the electricity in the room had jolted her, then crossed the room and swept aside the mess on Ethan's desk, settling the laptop on the polished wood. She lasered in on Meghan. "I'm guessing you're Meghan Mc-Guire?"

Meghan nodded and stepped around the desk, itching to dig through her computer to find something, some way to show she hadn't done anything illegal. Seeing her hard work—work she'd fought to protect—in a stranger's hands crawled all over her like spiders she couldn't brush away.

The woman smiled. "I'm Ashley Kincaid. And I think I found the first step to proving you're innocent."

FOURTEEN

If Meghan was the hugging type, she'd have thrown her arms around this stranger.

This stranger. The one Ethan Kincaid had loved enough to risk everything for.

Tate beat her to it, anyway. He wrapped an arm around Ashley's shoulder and laid a kiss on the top of her head. "I knew you could figure this out."

Ashley tossed him a wink, then motioned Meghan over, pointing to the screen where two separate windows sat open, Meghan's calendar and an operating system display. "This laptop never left your residence?"

"Once, when I moved it from my apartment to the house. I figured it was safer in the middle of nowhere. Security system was higher tech out there, because I could play with it, unlike at my apartment."

"And you never downloaded the program to another device until yesterday." The way Ashley said the words made them sound as though they were the most important Meghan would ever hear.

"I never even backed it up to another server. If the hard drive had died, it would all be gone, but I didn't want to risk someone else getting it." She pulled her attention from the screen to other woman. "What are we getting at?"

Ashley expanded the calendar and clicked to a date in last October. "You were at a conference in South Bend, Indiana, for three days."

"A teachers' convention." Three long days of classes with no way to escape. She remembered it well.

"You have proof?"

"I roomed with Yvonne, but seeing as how she's turned against me..."

"I can try to track your cell and see if it pinged a tower. Maybe I can locate some security footage. Anything would help at this point. We need to place you in South Bend on those dates." Ashley clicked to the other screen and pointed to a system file. "On that date, your file was transferred directly to a second laptop with a MAC address that's never been connected to you. The beauty is—" she winked, totally clueless to the dramatic pause she'd imposed "—I linked the laptop to your internet provider in Flint. They were on your internet at the same time, proof it was done at your residence."

Meghan leaned closer, her heart beating faster. "The laptop was in a small safe in my apartment." She turned to Ashley. "Can you track the computer?"

"Working on it now." Ashley slapped the laptop shut and pierced Meghan with a green-eyed gaze. "It's a thin piece of evidence, because there's no proof you didn't give someone permission to access your machine, but it's something." She grabbed Meghan's hand and squeezed. "I know Ethan's always trusted you. Tate, too. They believe in you, no matter how it might appear otherwise." One more squeeze and she was gone, leaving Meghan to wonder how someone investigating her could make her feel like her new best friend.

Hope dared to peek out from the closet where it had been hiding. Maybe she could get out of this. And maybe they'd find Phoenix and tear his plans apart once and for all.

Tate smiled a slow smile, then grew serious. "You want to talk this out?"

There was a small part of her that still wanted to punch him, but she nodded. "God's answer to prayer."

He froze, his green eyes sharp. "What?"

Meghan shrugged off the question. They could discuss her revelations later, when her brain wasn't in investigative mode. "Who accessed my machine while I was gone?"

It seemed as though Tate wasn't going to let her change the subject, but then he reluctantly paced away. "Maintenance workers? A break-in?" He was searching hard for her innocence, and she wasn't sure how to give it to him.

"The maintenance guys leave notes, and I don't remember getting one when I got home from Indiana."

"Roommate?"

"I've never…" Shock waved over her, weakening her knees. She reached for Tate and caught him by the arm.

"What?" Tate locked his hands under her elbows, holding on as if she'd thrown him a lifeline. "Meg?"

Meghan's gaze flickered around the room, seeking solid ground under a world rocking sideways. "Phoebe was working with lawyers to buy the farmhouse, and she stayed in my apartment while I was gone." *Phoebe.* Who knew she'd been a whiz with computers. Who had every reason to hate the military and all it stood for.

Tate pulled out his satellite phone and fired off a text.

Fighting a whole new pain, Meghan sank against the desk. Phoebe had been one of the few people she'd trusted. It couldn't be true. Phoebe was…Phoebe. No way could she be so devious. No way could she make so many plans with Meghan when the whole thing was a lie.

But memories of Phoebe's anger and bitterness over her brother's death, her actions in the aftermath… Everything said she could have done all of those things and much more.

The overwhelming magnitude of Phoebe's betrayal crashed like a tsunami threatening to suck Meghan out to sea.

Peace overran the pain, and she had no doubt where it came from. If she was going to trust, now was the time to start.

Meghan swiped at the thighs of her jeans, then straightened to her full height, ready for battle. But it was going to have to be God giving her the strength. Right now, all she wanted to do was rewind the clock and run away.

"Okay." She said, her mouth drawn into a grim line. "What do we do?"

"It's possible Phoenix is blackmailing her."

Meghan's chin lifted in defiance of her pain. She had to step into the place she'd lived in the army, the factual place where emotions didn't run the show. "No." She swallowed everything but reality, and it sat bitter in her mouth, coating words she hated to say. "I don't think there's blackmail involved. If she's working with him, it's voluntary."

The revelation had weight, and Tate's whole demeanor changed to his own fighting stance. "Why?"

"Her brother was killed in a friendly fire incident when we were sophomores in college. The military deemed it an accident. Phoebe was angry. She grieved hard. Our senior year, she pulled away from everybody. She organized antiwar protests, wrote papers on the dangers of government intervention in business..." Meghan stopped and balled her fists, nails digging into her palms. She'd missed it. She'd missed the most important clues ever laid out in front of her.

Ethan had been right. Emotions clouded your judgment, and she'd let it cloud everything she'd known about Phoebe Snyder. Meghan hadn't wanted to see one of the people she trusted most was not what she seemed. "Phoebe has all the marks, Tate. But I thought... We lost touch when I went into the army. When she contacted me to say she'd started the foundation and wanted me to work with them, I thought she was over it, that she'd found a way to take her grief and make it productive. She was happy."

"Wait." Tate's eyes narrowed as though he was reading something in the air. "Phoebe contacted you?"

"Yes."

"When?"

"I don't know exactly. About two years ago? We'd been in touch off and on, but she didn't contact me about the foundation until then."

"It was Thanksgiving last year when your program was used to hack Jessica Dylan's computer at Fort Campbell."

"Not long after I went to the conference in Indiana." Meghan felt as if her body was on fast forward while her mind swam in Jell-O. Her brain screamed a denial before shifting into hard knowing, an anger that swiped the pain aside in a violent flame. Meghan paced to the door. "She used me from the beginning." It had been a long time since she'd wanted to put her fist through something, but the door in front of her was in deep danger right now. "She played me. She knew I'd never be able to resist working with kids who were like me, kids who needed what I couldn't get. She built this whole facade to reel me in like a fish on a hook." Meghan leaned forward, digging her knuckles into the wood. She was supposed to be trained, too smart to allow someone to sucker her this way.

"She wasn't happier because she was healing. She was happier because she was doing something to tear at the fabric of the military."

Tate leaned against the wall beside Meghan and crossed his arms, bicep brushing hers. "Don't blame yourself for this."

"But I do." Meghan turned and mimicked his posture, her spine pressing against the door. "I was trained to notice these things." Memories poured in on a wave of self-doubt. "What I don't get is how she could possibly know what I did in the military. How would she know my skills were bigger than what I've always told her?"

"We suspected for a long time that Phoenix was working with the same mole who almost got me killed. It's possible Craig Mitchum found the connection between you two and Phoebe exploited it. The bigger question is how the two of them connected," Tate said. "What else?"

"When she first contacted me, she was about to buy

the house and was excited to get moving. She offered me enough money to allow me to work for her, but not so much that I asked questions. She spent several weekends at my place, planning how to make this work." Meghan's cramped apartment's walls had been covered with sticky notes and poster board, littered with ideas for sponsors and contacts...contacts Phoebe had probably used for their identities or for fraudulent donations to fund her horrible plans.

"And you thought nothing of her crashing at your place while she worked with the lawyer?"

Man, did shame ever burn. Meghan rubbed her stomach where a crater seemed to be forming. "I didn't keep the laptop as secure then. It was in a small digital keypad safe in the back of my closet, but with me being gone, she had time to get into it. I'd been working on the program the night before she arrived." Her long weekend away was probably enough time for Phoebe to snoop through her entire apartment. That was probably when she'd stumbled on Meghan's laptop and downloaded exactly what she needed.

"She targeted you because she knew you were good at what you do. Her skill set could only take her so far. She probably blackmailed you in college to give her more ammo to come at you with later." Tate scrubbed his chin before crossing his arms again, biceps tight against the sleeves of his gray T-shirt. "And you weren't involved?"

The question bristled along nerves already sensitive from the sting of betrayal and the burn of shame. Oh, logic knew why he had to ask, but her heart couldn't believe he was still hammering on her innocence.

"I was not involved." Along with the tenuous alibi

Ashley had found, her word and their history would have to be enough. Though she wondered, in the same position, if it would be enough for her.

Tate watched her, seeming to seek confirmation, before he pressed his lips together and nodded once. "Works for me."

She wanted to hug him, but she stopped herself, forcing her mind to work. Something was needling, digging, and until she could uncover it, restlessness ate at her. Meghan straightened, needing to move, to work the tension out of muscles so tight they felt as though they might snap.

And then...she knew what it was. Something she never wanted it to be. "What if she's not working for Phoenix?"

"I think it's pretty—"

Meghan cut him off with a wave. She didn't even want to think these thoughts, but with the lid of her life blown off, she was rational enough to consider every possibility, even the ones threatening to rip her into pieces. She sagged against Ethan's desk, the weight of revelation too heavy. "What if she is Phoenix?"

"Sit down, Walker. You're making me nervous." Sean Turner didn't turn from the laptop he was busy clicking away at. After terrorists kidnapped and tortured him, he'd left the military and now worked for Ashley's company, supporting the team as a civilian.

Tate stopped in the middle of the small dining room and stood with his hands at his sides, useless. Everything had gone to the tech side, his weak point.

The room had been converted into a makeshift command center. Sean Turner and Ashley Kincaid sat on opposite sides of the battered table, clicking through various databases, digging for ways to prove Meghan's innocence and Phoebe's guilt.

In the far corner, Meghan stood uncharacteristically silent and edgy, pulling at the hem of her T-shirt. Meghan had always been the one to comb through computers and deal with tracking hackers, tearing apart their systems while Tate provided the muscle.

Now both of them were helpless. As a suspect still, she wasn't allowed near a tech device. And as the brawn to everyone else's brains, Tate was no good unless someone kicked in the front door and launched a direct physical attack.

It was an unfamiliar sensation, being the one who had to wait for others to save the day. This was his job, not theirs. What good was he to anybody when all he could do was stand still?

He glanced at his watch for the hundredth time in the past hour, not even reading the numbers. Time didn't matter. They couldn't move until someone definitively linked Phoebe to Phoenix. "Where are we?"

Sean kept his attention on the screen before him. "Ashley's still combing Meghan's computer trying to find evidence she's not behind this. I started digging for intel on Phoebe the minute word came she might be our hacker. The girl's a ticking time bomb."

"Meghan said as much."

Meghan spoke for the first time since they'd walked into the room. "Phoebe has no computer training. Her lack of abilities might be our sticking point."

Tate turned from her to Sean, who shook his head. "Not true. After she graduated from college, she went back to school and studied computer science with a concentration in cybersecurity."

Meghan took a step closer to the table, her boldness returning to morph her into the familiar capable soldier who'd once been his partner. "When?"

"She finished about four years ago."

Right before Phoenix went active. Tate winced, watching Meghan. There it was then. They had every circumstantial piece of evidence in place. All they needed now was hard proof.

Meghan's eyes drifted closed, then opened again. This could not be easy for her. It was the second worst news she could get, next to continued proof of her own guilt. Probably she felt the same way he had when Ethan had laid out the evidence against Meghan to him. Betrayed. Hurt. Cut through the chest with an agony that eclipsed the pain of a literal knife.

He wanted to pull her close, but he was stuck in the middle of two worlds just as surely as he stood in the center of this room. This was his team, and she was still a suspect. No proof of her innocence had technically been found, although the team acted as though it existed.

He was also the outsider, the ghost who didn't officially live, who stood on the fringes and was called in when needed. A civilian, in the strict sense, playing at this military world. A civilian who could go to Meghan if he wanted.

And he wanted. Badly.

"Got it." Ashley punched a key with defiant force, and her laptop's display appeared on a large monitor on the far wall. She stood and jabbed a finger at the screen.

A list of numbers and letters that were nothing but

gibberish to Tate filled the screen. Here and there, he recognized an IP address or MAC address, but those were the extent of his knowledge.

But Meghan...she straightened and walked closer, pointing to a line near the bottom of the list. "You tracked the address of the computer that stole my file to an email address?"

Ashley nodded. "For a Robert Morgan. Know him?"

Ashley was in her element. The girl loved the thrill of the cyberhunt, even if she hated the guns that came with the other side of their unit's equation. If he'd taken a bullet the way she had when she was a military police officer, he'd probably be right there with her. He understood. The sight of a knife might not incapacitate him, but it sure did have a way of making him think twice.

Meghan's face tightened in a way Tate had seen. "Robert Morgan Snyder is Phoebe's brother. The one who was killed." She made the explanation to the room, though she continued to face the screen. Her eyebrows drew together in a deep V. "Find the date and the place."

"On it." Ashley went to work and within a few seconds had a news article on the screen.

The entire room fell silent.

Tate knew they were seeing exactly what he saw. The signature Phoenix had been using for years. The month, the initials of the town where Robert Snyder had been killed and the day.

Meghan turned to Tate. He knew exactly what she was thinking. How had she missed it? "You had no reason to look." He mouthed the reassurance to her, but it wouldn't make a difference. She'd beat herself with her perceived failure the same way he would.

"There's more to it." Ashley drew her lower lip between her teeth, watching her husband. "There have been email exchanges with someone at Leavenworth."

Fort Leavenworth. Where the army sent its worst criminals, including Ethan's former partner, Craig Mitchum, whose treachery had nearly killed them all at one point or another in this investigation.

The lines around Sean's mouth deepened as Ethan shoved away from the table and walked to the window, pounding the frame. "How? He's not supposed to have access to the outside."

"There are ways…" Ashley's voice tapered off.

Ethan reached for Ashley's, then looked at Sean. "We need to get someone at Leavenworth. Now."

Sean's voice cut into air mixed with triumph and anger. "I've got more first."

The back of Tate's neck tingled. Sean was either about to exonerate Meghan or put the final nail in her coffin.

Ethan asked the question none of them wanted to vocalize. "What else?"

"The Snyder Foundation doesn't exist."

"What?" Meghan sagged against the wall, her voice weak. "The house? The renovations?" *The kids?* She didn't say it, but the question hung there, punching Tate in the stomach with her confusion and her pain.

Sean wouldn't even look at them, his mouth pressed into a grim line. "No tax records, no mention in minutes from board meetings for the Snyders' corporation, no nothing."

"But I was paid…" Meghan's jaw went slack. "I was paid by direct deposit." Her shoulders drooped, and she stared at the ceiling. "Bank transfers to my account from Phoebe. Great. She thought this all the way through. Those transfers make me seem ten times guiltier."

Tate couldn't take anymore. Forget protocol and appearances. She needed him. He crossed the room in three strides and wrapped her in his arms.

She let him, sinking against his chest in a way uncharacteristic for her. In a way that spoke more about her anguish than anything else could. "There was no plan to help kids, was there?" Her voice was muffled into his shirt, and Tate doubted anyone else heard it. "I didn't even check her background. Me. The one who should have known better."

"She was your friend." He spoke against the wildness of her short dark hair. "You trust your friends."

"And look where that got me." She sniffed and pulled away, pressing her palms against her temples. "Who bought the house, Sean?"

He glanced at Ethan. "Robert Morgan."

"She stole her own brother's identity." Ethan released Ashley to stare at the big screen, even though Tate knew Ethan, like him, could understand about half of the information floating there.

"No." Meghan stepped away from Tate and ran her hands through her hair, standing it on end in a funky, punk-chick style. "This has always been about her brother. She didn't steal his identity. She's making a statement. She's avenging his death. She blames the military since it was friendly fire, even though it was an accident, a glitch with the computer system targeting the rocket that hit his platoon."

"Why come after us?" Ashley headed for her laptop, digging for more.

"Because we stopped her." Ethan strode to the window, back stiff. "She was aiding other terror cells, probably making exorbitant amounts of money to use when she decided how to turn on the military. She started years ago, exploited Meghan in college to make her first buck. She never used those identities because she didn't need them. She needed Meghan in her pocket, needed someone with her experience. The more she could pin on Meghan, the more she had to blackmail her with later. Meghan joining the military probably fueled Phoebe's fire, but it probably protected her from Phoebe coming at her sooner, too."

"How did she know I was hacking in high school?" Meghan moved around the table closer to Ethan and gripped the back of a chair.

"She ever meet any of your high school buddies?" Sean chimed in as he continued to comb databases.

"Once." Meghan winced. "Not long before I was blackmailed. It was right after her brother died and she started running wild. Had a…a fling with a guy I ran with in high school. He came to the college for a technology geek fest. He probably taught her a few computer tricks, too. He may even be the one who gave her the idea. He was shady, always trying to find a way to hack a big score."

Ashley sat poised over the keyboard. "Name?"

"Kenneth Schmidt."

Ashley started typing, tossing a comment to Sean. "You take private data—I'll take public."

Both dived into their work as Meghan tapped the table, clearly itching to take part.

Tate knew exactly how she felt.

"Guys?" Ashley stopped typing and punched a key,

pointing to the screen where a driver's license photo appeared.

"That's Kenneth," Meghan said.

"That's Craig Mitchum." Ethan walked to the screen and stared at it. "Hair's different, nose is different, but that's him." He balled his fist as though he might put it through the screen. "He's smarter than he acted. I'm going to go out on a limb and say he's been behind this all along."

"And he's using Phoebe as his puppet." Ashley drummed her keyboard, staring at the screen, her face paling.

Tate was pretty sure she'd never wanted to see Mitchum's face again.

"Or Phoebe's using him." Ethan slid a piece of paper closer and started writing, plotting out their theories. "We know Mitchum wasn't hacking the military's computers for Sam Mina, so it had to be Phoebe behind him getting Mina more money than his contracts were worth, funding cell overseas."

"Mitchum was already locked away when we started working the op in Kentucky." Sean stopped typing. "It had to be Phoebe who talked Mina into going after us. I don't think it's too much of a stretch to guess stealing soldiers' identities to put sleeper cells in place wasn't Mina's son's idea. He wasn't bright enough."

"The idea was all Phoenix." Ethan knocked his knuckles on the table. "Phoebe was tracking our every move then, drawing us in to try to take us out at the same time. She got more vengeful then."

"Because we put Mitchum away." Tate didn't have to search far to figure that one out. He'd been ready to scrap his reputation for Meghan. If Mitchum and Phoebe were working together, anything could happen.

"But she failed." Sean went to his work, his mouth a grim line.

"Then what's her plan now?" Meghan paced to the window, staring out at the wind-whipped trees, the late afternoon sun highlighting her anguish.

"It's no good, whatever it is." Ashley swiped the touch pad on her laptop, and the wall display changed to a news story. "Phoebe Snyder's vanished."

FIFTEEN

The heat of summer dampened in the woods as Meghan stepped over a root on the narrow path leading to the river, Tate following close behind. The wind blew high, rustling the leaves on the trees and drowning out the rush of the water nearby.

She'd had to get out of the room, to get into clear air filled with the earthy scent of fresh leaves and river mud. Nothing else would clear the sewage churning in her mind. Phoebe was in league with their bad guy, and now she'd vanished. Her car had been abandoned near the farmhouse. The police now combed the scene. It wouldn't be long before Meghan and Tate were the lead story on the six o'clock news.

Meghan swiped a branch from her face and kept moving. Maybe physical exertion would clear her mind. The future didn't matter if they couldn't figure out what was going on in the present. Either Phoebe was Phoenix and this was getting worse by the second, or Phoebe was another pawn, like Isaac and his gang, easily annihilated when her usefulness was tapped.

If the trail was wider, Meghan would've run. Run

until she passed out, forgetting everything for a few blessed black moments.

Planting her feet in the middle of the trail, Meghan inhaled damp air and let the distant rush of water wash over her as the leaves rattled above. For half a second, she'd choose the lie of denial. For half a second, she'd block out reality and believe everything would be fine when she opened her eyes again. She'd let herself get lost in the if-onlys she never allowed herself to explore, the ones that could have made all of this go away.

If only she'd told Tate her feelings instead of running away. If only he'd felt the same way. If only…

So many variables had led them to this path. If things had been different, this could have been any given summer afternoon, the two of them hiking through the woods on a lazy afternoon getaway.

Except it wasn't any given afternoon. And Tate's presence with her now was muddy. Was he here because he wanted to be? Or, despite what they said, because nobody trusted her to be out of sight?

"That was a huge sigh." Tate stepped beside her on the narrow trail, so close his arm brushed hers.

She wanted to grab him and hold on tight, but no matter what he said or did, she wasn't totally certain her heart would ever trust anyone again. Ethan had gone against his own counsel after derailing her shot at happiness. Tate had been dead to her while he was really alive. And Phoebe…

There it was again, the peace she couldn't define, the reminder of the way she'd promised to give everything to the only one who couldn't break His promise never to leave her.

Okay, Lord. I can do this. But You have to help me.

As damaged as she was right now, there was no way she could have faith on her own.

Meghan swallowed the pain knifing her in the throat, hoping for the kind of peace she'd felt earlier. "You've got moxie bringing me out here, you know." She winced at her choked voice, wishing it had more force, more levity.

"Yeah?"

"Yeah. You've seen me in action. You know what I'm capable of. For all you know, I'll bolt into the woods and you'll never find me." If it wouldn't make her look like a sure suspect, she'd consider it. It wouldn't be hard to find a new life far away from hackers and suspicion and friends who played at betrayal in the worst of ways.

Tate wrapped his fingers around hers and stepped in front of her, drawing her closer. "You'd never do it."

Lifting her chin, Meghan found him looking right at her, once again searching for something she couldn't even begin to imagine.

It was a comfort she couldn't let herself fall into. Not when she had questions digging claws into every thought. "What if we let Phoebe walk into a trap?"

"I know this is hard, but you're grasping at straws." Tate cupped her face, his touch warm against her skin, and brushed her cheek with his thumb. "Phoebe's not innocent. If she walked into anything at the house, it was something of her own doing. *Think, Meg.* She breezed in yesterday morning, saw I was still there and gave herself time to get away before the shooting started."

"I don't want any of it to be true. If it's true, then she's a liar and I'm an idiot. I'm a stupid, easily manipulated idiot." Resentment charged her pulse, and she stared at the gray T-shirt stretching over Tate's chest.

How had he moved past Stephanie's betrayal of their marriage vows and reached the place where he could pray for her, could have concern for her soul after what she did?

How could Tate have reached a place where he could kiss Meghan the way he had last night, pouring everything into her in a way that said he wasn't crushed and broken?

Meghan laid her hand over his heart. It really did still beat. After physical brutality and emotional destruction, it still thumped a steady rhythm in his chest. Such a feat had to be impossible.

But Meghan knew there was one explanation. "God."

"What?" Tate's low question rumbled against her touch.

Meghan swallowed, wishing she'd not let her deepest thoughts slip but unable to turn back now, not without answers. "You trust God. He helped you survive."

"He did." Tate let his hands drift across her shoulders to her back, capturing her hand between them, his heart still beating against her palm.

She slipped her arms around him, desperate for his peace to flow through her. "I realized this morning you're right. When I go back over my life, I can see where I've been wrong, where God's been there all along but, boy… He didn't wait to test my faith, did He?"

Tate's arms tightened around her, and he laid a kiss above her ear, murmuring something into her hair that had to be a prayer, washing over her in a way that made her feel safer than she ever had.

Which was dangerous if they were going to end the threat to their lives.

Meghan held him close, then stepped away, breaking the connection between them but hanging on to the peace she'd found in his prayers and in his arms.

He seemed reluctant to let her go, his caress trailing across her back and down her arms before disconnecting when he reached her fingertips.

If Meghan didn't get some distance soon, she'd suggest they keep walking until they vanished into the woods and no one ever found them. Both of them had disappeared before. It wouldn't be hard.

"If Phoebe really is Phoenix or a minion, then why come after me? Why waste so much time and effort coaxing me into being her friend?" The hurt lingered, pinching her soul, even as peace coated her spirit.

Tate acted as though he'd rather do anything other than dive into this discussion, but he put some space between them, watching the trees for a long beat before his face hardened. "Did she know about me? Did she know I was your partner?"

"To an extent. I told her the guy I… I told her a guy I worked with and was close to was killed."

"You told her my name?"

"Yes."

Tate pivoted on one heel and walked to the edge of the path. "The op in Kentucky, when we put a hurt on Mina's son and stopped those sleeper cells… I was all over the place. I was on post after they detonated Sean's car. I was on the insertion team when we went in to take Mina out and rescued Jessica Dylan. I was at her house the whole time we were working. Wouldn't take much to find out who I was, especially the way Phoenix was listening in the whole time."

"If she's taking care of her loose ends, it might make

sense to come after me since she drew me in when she first started, but that can't be it. She could have taken me out anytime she wanted. There has to be something more. She used me as bait to draw you in and kept you in when Isaac came after me." Meghan closed the gap and turned Tate toward her, trying to communicate the urgency of her next question. If she was right…"Is there anybody on the team who isn't here?"

"Nobody." His expression hardened with realization. "She's got all of us together, in one place." Tate pulled his phone from his pocket and turned toward the house. "I think we figured out her endgame."

"Come on." Tate pressed Send and, once again, the text to Ethan failed to go through. He'd already tried to call twice, but the calls had tanked, as well.

Meghan leaned closer to the screen, then turned toward the sky. "It's windy, but there's no reason for your sat phone to be out."

Typically, Ashley let them know ahead of time if sunspot activity or satellite issues were going to be a problem, but she'd said nothing lately. No, something else was on.

Something a whole lot worse.

"Your signal's jammed." Meghan turned toward the house. "Either Phoebe's here or someone doing her dirty work is."

There was no other explanation. She'd herded them together and her final move started now. No chance to plan, no chance to warn the team, no idea what they were pitted against.

They pushed along the narrow path, a branch thwacking back to catch Tate on the cheek. He swiped at the spot, blood smearing across his fingers, but he kept going, determined to stay a step ahead of Meghan. No way was she going in ahead of him, unarmed and alone.

At the edge of the safe house's small yard, they stopped, dropping into the thick foliage at low ground. The afternoon sun glared against the windows, making it impossible to detect movement in the dining room where they'd left the team. The house sat on stilts, lifting it high to give it ample views of the trees and river and to guard against potential flooding. Right now, the view straight through gave Tate a clear line of sight to the other side of the house. Nothing moved in the yard or the woods anywhere around them.

"Think we might have been wrong?" Meghan leaned close, her voice low and backed by the rush of the wind through the trees.

"No." There was no way his satellite phone had coincidentally stuttered at the penultimate moment in their investigation. Tate didn't believe in coincidence, and neither did Meghan. Instinct had kept them both alive in odd moments around the globe when the endings should have been different. He clenched and unclenched his fists. Outside of the wind in the trees, nothing was moving, and that wasn't right. "I don't think we were wrong."

"Oh, you were right."

Tate whipped toward the voice as Meghan turned with him. Reaching for the gun concealed at his hip, Tate found himself eye-to-barrel with another pistol about six feet away. He steeled himself from recoiling, refusing to let anyone see him back away an inch. In one quick glance, he took in the young blonde woman with a firm aim at his head. They had numbers on their side, but he wasn't quite ready to chance going for his gun, not unless Phoebe's aim wavered. If he kept still, she may not realize he had it. He could wait her out for a bit, unless she decided to pull the trigger.

"Phoebe." Meghan's choked utterance carried toward the house with the wind that had covered Phoebe's approach. "What are you doing?"

Meghan's voice sounded helpless, but Tate knew better. The innocence she'd played so many times came edged into the forefront. His partner wasn't going down without trying her level best to find out all she could on the way.

Tate gauged the distance between Phoebe and himself, almost certain he could neutralize her before she could fire. But a motion in the foliage behind Phoebe to the left stopped him, and a man stepped out, holding an AR-15 rifle low.

The numbers tilted to balance, but now they were outgunned and Tate felt the rush of adrenaline from knowing the fight was on. He was pretty sure Phoebe didn't realize he had the weapon on him, or she'd have disarmed him already. If she wavered and he drew fast enough, he could handle her and get a shot off at her partner before the rifle could lift and sight. He edged sideways slowly, maneuvering for the best position.

"I'd stay still if I were you." Phoebe took a calculated step back, keeping herself out of arm's reach as the man behind her raised his rifle. "It's killing you how you can't play hero right now, I'm sure." She smiled. "From what I've seen, swooping in to save the day is what you do best." Her smile widened, hard and colder than the eyes of the man who'd slaughtered Isaac's gang. "I almost feel sorry for you, because today's not going to be your day." She shifted her attention to Meghan. "And you. I've seen your service record, and you are nowhere near the innocent you like to pretend to be."

"You can't bring Robert back." Meghan didn't drop the facade. "Why do all of this?"

Phoebe's nostrils flared slightly. "My brother is off the table for discussion, and you don't get to ask the questions. This isn't a movie, and you won't get me dialoguing." She dipped the gun and aimed squarely at Tate's chest, a more stable target than his head.

A little bit of Tate's confidence dipped. Someone had schooled her in aiming for center mass. She knew what she was doing.

Phoebe tipped her head toward the house. "Both of you stand and start walking. If one of you gets brave, I kill the other one. I know how you feel about Tate Walker, Meghan. I wouldn't push me on this one. As quiet as you are, that night over dinner was one time you talked entirely too much for your own good." She jerked her chin toward the clearing. "Let's go."

There was nothing to do for the moment but to obey. Tate hoped for even a brief moment of eye contact with Meghan and a chance to form a plan before the situation deteriorated further. From the shoot-out at the house, they already knew Phoebe had at least two men in her hip pocket, and there was no telling what had happened to her muscle from last night. There was a high likelihood that, somewhere on the property, at least one more adversary lurked.

Having no intel made Tate's stomach tighten. Without knowledge, he couldn't wrestle back control.

Keeping a wary gaze on Phoebe, Tate jerked a thumb

at the house. "You know the minute we step out of the woods we're in full view of everybody inside."

"Your team won't matter in a minute."

A jolt of adrenaline shot pain through Tate. If he hadn't been trained to hide his thoughts, he'd have doubled over. With sudden clarity, he knew where Phoebe's second lackey was.

And there was nothing he could do to stop what was coming. His team, the next best thing he had to family, was in danger and had no idea the hit was coming, that Phoebe had a second man with them in his sights. His muscles ached to run, to shout, but he'd never get far enough and they'd never hear him from this distance.

They were going to die…and he couldn't stop it.

"You're going to kill us all?" He fought to sound strong, to maintain a front and cover the rage and fear simmering inside him. He'd stop this. There had to be a way. He'd always managed to stop it before and this time could be no different.

"No." Phoebe's blue eyes pierced his. "Unless Meghan does something stupid, you get to live. As long as you're alive but in danger, Meghan has the motivation to do whatever I ask. The rest of your team? They die. And Meghan comes with me, because you've all made it complicated to communicate with my partner in prison. The only way you die is if Meghan doesn't cooperate." She flicked a glance at the house and pinned Tate again. "I'd much prefer you live knowing you couldn't save them and you couldn't save her."

Across the lawn, a volley of gunfire exploded; windows in the house shattered and cascaded outward. There were two more shots, then a third before the voice of the wind reigned once again.

SIXTEEN

For all of Meghan's training—after all she'd seen in the field—nothing had prepared her for hearing the team slaughtered. She'd barely grasped Phoebe's intent when the shots rang out, a one-two punch to her gut.

She jumped at the shots and the showering glass, whirling toward the house with the instinct to run toward the family who needed her.

Her shoulder collided with Tate's, knocking them both sideways, her wrist crashing into the pistol at his hip. For the briefest instant, his eyes caught hers.

And she gave her tight-lipped agreement.

Phoebe had proven herself to be the coldhearted killer Meghan hadn't wanted to admit she was. The weight of accumulated grief—for the death of trust, the pain of deceit and the murder of friends new and old—knotted in resolve. She turned a hard gaze on the woman who'd betrayed her. "You want me to come with you?"

Phoebe nodded. "Exactly. Because of your former teammates, Kenneth's no longer easily accessible…" Her voice dropped and something similar to grief clouded her vision before she refocused on Meghan.

"His absence is your fault. Both of your faults. So you get to be my new partner." She held the gun with an unwavering aim at Tate. "And you get to suffer."

"You ought to know I'll never help you." Meghan edged a half inch closer to Tate, until she was within arm's length of him.

"You don't come with me, I shoot him in front of you." Phoebe steadied the pistol. "We're in the middle of our own little operation and—"

"Shutting the power off to the whole country isn't an op. It's insanity," Tate said. He was trying to keep Phoebe talking long enough for Meghan to get into position. "Where do you think you're going to run? You'll cascade a—"

"Not every country in the world needs ours, Tate. I've got plenty of places to take refuge. And, Meghan, if you come on board and prove useful, you get to go free. But if you get smart and come with me now, then try to refuse later? Well, I think you already know I can track Tate anywhere he runs. I've already turned your own program against you and found you here. Finding him will be easy. And I'll make sure to give you a front-row seat to the aftermath." She waved, signaling her silent partner. "Disarm him." She kept her attention on Tate. "And if you go for his gun, Meghan, every single deal is off the table and Tate dies now."

Beside her, Tate tensed, a clear indication of what was coming.

Meghan readied herself to move when he did.

When Phoebe's henchman stepped into range, Tate charged, catching the other man in the stomach and driving him backward. The pair slammed against a tree as the rifle fired, throwing dirt and dust between Phoebe and Meghan.

In the instant Phoebe's attention turned, Meghan leaped forward, catching Phoebe in the chest and shoving her to the ground, the gun flying into the woods behind her. Meghan scrambled, throwing her arm across Phoebe's neck and driving her chin up, pinning her head at an awkward position into the ground, cutting off the other woman's air as she fought to pin Phoebe's arms with her knees.

Hard metal drove into her side, lodging against her ribs.

Phoebe glared and rasped out, "I will...pull...the trigger."

Breathing hard, Meghan dug her arm in deeper to Phoebe's neck, but the pressure against her ribs increased, as well, the threat clear in Phoebe's expression.

Meghan dropped her hold, falling to a crouch as Phoebe stood. Waiting for an opportunity to seize the small pistol Phoebe had concealed, Meghan tried to take in everything around her at once. From her awkward position with her back to Tate and the other shooter, there was no way to gain the advantage.

"Tate." Phoebe's voice rang off the trees. "I can find another Meghan if you force me to do away with this one."

The sounds of struggle stopped.

"No more talk." Phoebe spoke to the men behind Meghan. "Take Walker to the house and make sure he can't deny his guilt in the murder of his team. Drop the evidence from Saginaw in there, as well, so he can take the rap for Isaac, too." She gestured for Meghan to make a wide circle and start walking toward the house.

"I'm out of patience. Either of you tries to get out of this again, and I give up on you both."

They marched onto the lawn, Tate walking a few feet from her on the right. She didn't dare look at him. If she did, she'd crumble. Everything Ethan had said was true. She'd sacrifice herself right now if she thought it would save him. Every scenario she considered was overshadowed by the truth he could die if she failed. Her judgment was clouded, her mind racing, and she had about a hundred feet before they'd be separated and she'd have no idea of his fate. For all she knew, he'd be dead as soon as he was out of her sight, a ghost Phoebe could hold over her forever.

She put all her focus on the grass before her, trying to set her mind to a plan. Phoebe had to be taking her to a vehicle. There was at least one other shooter they had yet to see. Meghan would bide her time, wait for an opening when Tate was no longer close, and she could take out Phoebe without fearing Tate would get caught in the cross fire.

The same as the rest of the team. Meghan lifted her face toward the shattered windows at the rear of the small house. How had it come to this? No matter what she gained in an escape, the carnage was already heinous, a weight she'd carry to the grave.

At the closest window, something flashed, then vanished.

Meghan's foot hesitated. What was…?

A force caught her from the side, driving her into the ground as shots blasted over the howl of the wind in the trees. She hit the ground with a crash that forced the air from her lungs, body tensed against the thud of a bullet as the back of her head smacked the sun-warmed grass, ringing her ears and shooting stars across her vision.

"Meg." The voice came from far away, and Meghan fought darkness to grab onto it. Shaking her head against the pain in the back of her neck, she forced her eyes open.

Tate leaned over her, running his hands over her face, her shoulders. "You're okay?"

She was okay if he was. "Did you have to tackle me like a linebacker?"

His grin arched half of his mouth upward. "I had to tackle you if you wanted to be out of the way of Sean and Ethan's sharpshooting."

They were alive? Meghan struggled to sit up, but Tate's gentle pressure on her shoulders wouldn't let her. "Everybody's good?"

The grim ache in Tate's eyes shifted as running feet drew closer. "Our team is. They signaled from the window and got the high sign from me before they fired. Phoebe was cocky enough to think her guy had finished the job. She paid for that assumption." He eased Meghan into a sitting position, placing himself in front of her to block her view of what lay beyond him. "She won't be giving us any answers." He planted a kiss to her forehead and pulled her close. "I'm sorry, Meg."

The shaking started from somewhere inside and radiated outward until Tate had to be able to feel it. The Phoebe she thought she'd known had never existed. And the Phoebe who held the answers to all of her questions lay dead a few feet away. Despite the fact the woman had tried to kill her, had manipulated the most important dream in her life, Meghan couldn't stop the wave of sadness at a life and death so horribly twisted and destroyed.

Tate didn't try to make anything better, didn't try to explain the grief away. He simply held her to him, doing that thing he did where his touch was bigger than his words, his presence more than enough to soothe the broken places.

Sean approached, weapon drawn and aimed at their fallen suspects. "You guys okay?"

Meghan would have to grieve later. Right now, she had too many unanswered questions. "What happened?" Meghan pulled away from Tate, but kept a hand on him, her anchor in a world spinning from her impact with the ground. "We heard—"

"Ashley's smarter than the average bear." Sean crouched beside Tate, favoring his right knee. "She has cameras on the driveway, so we were ready when Phoebe's friend came in. It was you guys we were worried about."

Ethan approached, his silhouette blocking the sun as he stood over them. "We didn't want to risk an on-ground firefight. That would have leveled the playing field and put you two in the cross fire. We had to wait for you to get clear before we could take a shot. Thought it would never happen."

"It's over?" From the ringing in her ears, Meghan wasn't sure which of the men asked the question.

It was Tate who answered. "Once we make sure Mitchum's communication is cut off."

"Already on it," Sean said. He stood slowly and held a hand out to Meghan, pulling her to her feet before turning to Tate and offering him a hand up, as well. "I need to talk to you, Walker." He aimed a finger toward the house. "Without ears."

Tate cast Meghan a look that reeked of regret before he stepped away, leaving her alone with Ethan.

She refused to look at Phoebe's fallen body, turning to face the house instead. "Now what?"

"Now we finish clearing your name. It's preliminary, but after you walked out, Ashley and Sean both agreed they couldn't find a trace of anything linking you to Phoenix other than the program and the bank transfers, which might be complicated but can be explained." Ethan walked around to stand between Phoebe and the house, forcing her to pay attention to him. "Listen, I need to say something to you. Higher's on the way and they'll separate us for debrief, so I might not get another chance."

"You really—"

"No, I do." Ethan tapped his fingers on his chest. "I kept you in the dark about Tate. Yeah, it was operational and need to know, but still...and before that. Meghan, I steered you wrong, let my own experience get in the way of what you needed to hear. Everybody's different, and I warned you away from Tate, thinking I was doing you a favor." He glanced at Tate and Sean, talking on the other side of the yard. "I'm sorry."

"You were right." She couldn't let him take the heat for her choices. "You gave me advice, and I didn't have to follow it. I chose to run because I was scared, and that's not your fault. You were the excuse."

"Now what?" Ethan echoed her earlier question.

"Good question." One Meghan didn't have an answer to. She watched Tate as he talked, his posture saying he was in this game until the end, whenever that may be.

And after that? He'd probably be in the wind again on an op, as unreachable as ever. She'd never ask him to deny the life he loved to settle down with her. So, now what?

She had no idea.

Her cup of coffee long cold, Meghan sat on the front steps of the farmhouse where her dreams had once lived and studied the dark driveway, where a rogue piece of yellow police tape fluttered from a tree. She'd spent the late afternoon and evening boarding up the front windows and fighting off a restless sadness that refused to be shaken.

A tactical team had swept the area around the Virginia safe house and discovered an SUV containing Phoebe's laptops and servers, which Ashley had started combing as soon as she could get them. After a once-over by the paramedics, the team had been separated and driven to Washington for debriefing.

Meghan had been questioned for hours then detained for two days until Ashley was able to prove Meghan hadn't been working with the enemy. Cell phone records and computer hard drives had yielded a gold mine against Phoebe and Craig Mitchum. There had also been enough to send several Special Forces teams in to put a stop to the cells who'd aligned with Phoenix to destroy the power grid.

When no evidence implicating Meghan was found, she'd flown alone to Michigan, arriving at the farmhouse early in the afternoon, wanting to say goodbye before she returned to Flint to pack her apartment and went…where?

She'd battled within herself, spent hours in a small room with a cot and a TV at headquarters praying. For herself, for Tate…for the hurt to go away and to be able to forgive. For God to help her do whatever came next. And to let go of the love she was pretty sure would never diminish for Tate Walker.

But they'd have to. Since he'd been separated from her at the house, there hadn't been a word. Her cell phone lying on the steps beside her had been silent, save a call from Yvonne with an apology as big as the other woman's heart. Phoebe's blackmail was horrific, the threat to Yvonne's family terrifying. She'd issued an invitation for Meghan to return to the school, but Meghan's heart wasn't with the school.

It was still here. In this house, with kids who needed her. But even though her savings account was large, it wasn't large enough to fund the start-up of a home like this one.

Staying here was impossible, anyway. Despite the fact that he'd only spent a single day on the farm, the property leaked memories of Tate. Because at some point along the way, he'd become part of the dream. Maybe had been all along.

Thinking was getting her nowhere. Meghan drained her cold coffee and stood, determined to sleep tonight, unlike the previous night or the night before.

Headlights cut through the trees. Setting her cup on the rail, Meghan waited, tense, still not quite convinced life was safe again.

A Jeep pulled closer and stopped at the edge of the clearing. The headlights flickered three times, paused, then flashed twice more.

Tate.

Not sure whether to cry or laugh, Meghan froze on

the top step. Her heart beat harder, shooting electricity to her toes. Just when she'd decided it was finished…

He climbed out of the Jeep, his silhouette dark against the trees, and crossed the yard without the hesitation he'd harbored a few nights ago. He looked the exact same yet…different, as though the past week had changed him.

"'Bout time you got here." Meghan winced when the words choked on emotion she wasn't ready to reveal.

"Didn't realize we had a date." He stopped at the foot of the stairs, his black T-shirt making his green eyes brighter than ever. They focused exclusively on her. "Unless you're telling me I have a standing invitation?"

He could have whatever he wanted, but not knowing where things stood, she swallowed the sentiment. He was probably there to say goodbye before he headed off on another mission. Flitting around the world was what he did. And he did it well. She'd never take his passion from him. "Where's the next destination? Or is it classified?"

Something similar to amusement flickered in his expression, and it hit Meghan what was different. The lines around his mouth had almost vanished, as though a tension had released. And looking at her now, something in his expression softened even more. "As it turns out, there was a reward for anyone giving us enough information to stop Phoenix for good."

"A reward." Her heart picked up speed. Was he saying what she thought he was saying?

"It's a big one." He stepped one step closer to her. "Big enough to make dreams come true for a whole lot of kids who could use some dreams of their own. And it's yours."

Meghan's breath caught in her throat. Her hand went to her mouth. "I can still—"

"You can still start the foster home. And, if I'm any good at math at all, you can run it for a long time."

Tears she hadn't even felt coming broke through and coursed down her cheeks; prayers she hadn't even dared to speak were answered right in front of her. She sniffed. There was still one unspoken prayer. "What about you?"

Tate climbed the final step, and the heat of him telegraphed to her, his hooded gaze drifting to her lips, then to her eyes. "You tell me." His hands eased to her sides, warm through her thin T-shirt, releasing a shiver to wrap around her spine and drop her stomach like the best kind of carnival ride.

"What's that supposed to mean?"

He slipped his arms around her, pulling her against him, his lips brushing her temple before easing to her ear. "I need a job."

Meghan could hardly breathe. "What kind?" The question didn't even qualify as a whisper.

He pulled away enough to smile into her eyes. "Something permanent. Like…till-death-do-us-part permanent." He leaned closer, his lips a whisper from hers. "Know of anything?"

There was no need to respond. Meghan closed the gap, pulling him closer, losing herself in a kiss that promised her the world they'd already seen together. That promised her the future they weren't supposed to have…and the dreams that were finally coming true.

EPILOGUE

Meghan leaned against a porch post and crossed her arms, watching the progress on the backyard. The paint fumes in the den where she'd been working with some of the wives from the volunteer fire department left her needing a good dose of fresh air. The Saturday after Thanksgiving was chilly; the air cleared her head and reminded her how much she truly had to be thankful for.

Tate had gathered their small circle of friends to help on the holiday weekend as they put the final touches on the house. There was still plenty of legal red tape to push through, but soon they'd have their own foundation for foster children. One they'd run here, together.

The thought of starting "forever" with Tate in this house still thrilled in her stomach. She ran her thumb along the back of the ring he'd presented her on the Fourth of July. The sooner the house was finished, the sooner they could abandon their separate apartments, finally plan a wedding and move in here together.

So much change in the past few months. It still amazed her, all that Tate had brought to her life in these few short months. Changes that included a whole new kind of family.

Aside from the women in the living room, there was a crew from the school painting bedrooms upstairs. The youth from the church Tate and she now attended were busy at the far end of the backyard, stacking stones around a brick-lined fire pit. In the kitchen, Ethan, Ashley, Sean and his fiancée, Jessica, were painting cabinets and walls, having stayed on after a celebratory Thanksgiving dinner a couple of days before.

On the opposite side of the yard, the skeleton of a gazebo stood abandoned, the volunteer firemen away answering a call.

Meghan grinned. For all of Tate's need to settle down, a small part of him still sought to help others—and to chase the occasional adrenaline rush—and he'd found his place in the volunteer fire department that protected their community.

The porch floor creaked behind her. "You've got paint on your forehead." Tate's voice ran the best kind of cold chills along her arms.

He appeared at her right shoulder and swiped his thumb across her skin, showing her the proof before swiping the paint onto his jeans.

She leaned into his chest, letting him bear her weight, still shocked at how easy it had been to trust him once she'd let God work on the broken places inside. There were still times when she needed reassurance, but the more days that passed, the fewer those moments became. "You're back fast."

"False alarm."

"Hmm." She laid her hands against his chest, firm beneath his sweatshirt, and enjoyed the feel of being near him for a moment. But then she straightened and eyed something near the fire pit, something that was definitely out of place. "Tate? Why's there a six-foot penguin in the yard? Dressed like a firefighter?" All work on the fire pit had stopped as the youth lined up to laugh at and high-five some sort of huge penguin mascot.

Tate laughed, running a hand down her arm, leaving a warm shiver behind. "Funny story about that."

"Do tell."

"That's Joe. He's a volunteer in the next town over. I was on my way back from the call when I saw this… this penguin wearing turnout gear standing beside the road next to an old pickup."

"This sounds like the start of a very bad joke."

"Yeah, but it's true." He planted a kiss on the top of her head. "He was at one of the churches doing a program on fire safety and how the kids shouldn't be afraid of firemen in gear, even though they can look scary. His station got the same call we did, so he took off still suited up, but his truck broke down and here we are."

"He came to entertain the kids? They're a bit old for that." Still, it was cute watching Joe the Firefighting Penguin pretend to direct the fire pit build while the kids saluted. Laughter drifted across the yard as Joe kept up the game. He kept looking their way though, as if he was more interested in the happenings on the porch than in the yard.

"No." Tate shook his head, eyes taking on that spark that said he was about to bring on some sort of new surprise. "He's actually here for something else."

"To teach you not to pick up strangers by the side of the road?"

"I've told you before—you're not half as funny as you think you are." Tate pulled her to stand in front of him and wrapped his arms around her waist, his green eyes boring into hers. "Joe's a preacher. Young kid, fresh out of seminary."

"And?" She was having trouble following. When he looked at her like that, it made her want to drag him to the nearest courthouse to get married right then. She'd held out so far, but she wasn't sure either of them could live apart much longer.

"And all of our friends are here."

Something in his voice tweaked at her heart, amping up the beat to double time. "And?"

"And in the state of Michigan, it only takes one party to go to the courthouse and get a marriage license issued."

Meghan tried to back away from him, but he held tight. "What are you saying?" *And please let it be what I think it is.*

"That since the house is pretty much finished, I had this grand plan to drive you up to Mackinac Island and marry you before Christmas. I took your ID last week and got a license, but…" He let his gaze sweep hers, then the yard around them. "But now I'm thinking you and I have never been close to normal. And you? You never got to do all of those great kiddo things like going to theme parks and meeting all of those cartoon characters the rest of us grew up with. We have our family here and we have Joe the Firefighting Penguin Preacher here and…" When his eyes came back to hers, they were burning with the kind of fire she'd always wanted to dive into. "And I'm very, very sure I don't want to wait another minute." He dipped his head and brushed a kiss over her lips, whispering against them. "So what do you say, McGuire? Marry me right this minute in this wreck of a backyard in your paint-stained blue jeans?"

Nothing in her whole life had ever sounded so right. Meghan knit her fingers together behind the back of Tate's head and pulled him lower, answering him with a kiss that promised him the craziest wedding in the world…and every crazy day for the rest of her life.

* * * * *

If you enjoyed this exciting story of
military suspense and intrigue,
pick up these other stories from Jodie Bailey

FREEFALL
CROSSFIRE
SMOKESCREEN
COMPROMISED IDENTITY

Available now from Love Inspired Suspense!

Find more great reads at www.LoveInspired.com

Dear Reader,

I hope you enjoyed Tate and Meghan's story! These two gave me some serious fits and starts. Tate kept insisting he had no flaws that he knew of. Meghan kept telling me she didn't need anybody's help. For a while, they refused to work together at all. But when the characters finally let me wrangle them, they showed up on the page like no others. They may just be my favorites. I think Meghan just didn't want the world to know about her past.

We all have a past, don't we? I am fond of saying, "If we all got together and talked about the worst things we've ever done, it would probably curl all of our hair." It's true. We all have that something we're not proud of, and sometimes we let our past stand in the way of our future.

Like Meghan, some of us try to bury history. This is the thing I've learned: the more we try to bury it, the more it controls us. When we bring it into the light, the most amazing thing happens. It's no longer the driving force in our lives and, if we let Him, God will use it to do amazing things. Things we can't even conceive. We just have to be brave enough to hand Him the controls.

The driving verse for Tate and Meghan's story was Isaiah 43:18–19. I love it when God says, "See? I am doing a new thing!" Or in 2 Corinthians 5:17: "The old is gone, the new is here!" It's there again in Revelation 21:5: "I am making everything new!" (Love how there is always an exclamation point, like God's excited about it. He is, you know.) Over and over again, God lets us know He is all about making us new, not who we used to be, but the brilliance of who we could be. That is one of my favorite things about Jesus. And thank God He sees the new and not the old!

I would love to hear from you! You can find me on the web at www.jodiebailey.com or email me at jodie@jodiebailey.com. Maybe you've got a story about how God's "made all things new" with you. Seems to be the story of my life.

Happy reading!
Jodie Bailey

COMING NEXT MONTH FROM
Love Inspired® Suspense

Available October 4, 2016

IDENTITY UNKNOWN
Northern Border Patrol • by Terri Reed
When Nathanial Longhorn washes up on deputy sheriff Audrey Martin's beach—followed by men intent on killing him—he has no memory. And Audrey is the only one he trusts to protect him as he recovers his past.

HIGH-RISK REUNION
Lone Star Justice • by Margaret Daley
Someone is out for revenge against district attorney Tory Carson. And they're willing to hurt her teenage daughter to get to her. But Tory's former love, Texas Ranger Cade Morgan, will do whatever it takes to keep them both safe.

LAKESIDE PERIL
Men of Millbrook Lake • by Lenora Worth
Chloe Conrad suspects foul play in the plane crash that killed her sister—and she hires private investigator Hunter Lawson to prove it. But when their investigation puts both of their lives in jeopardy, can they find the truth before they become the next victims?

TARGETED FOR MURDER
Wilderness, Inc. • by Elizabeth Goddard
Chased by assassins after her secret agent father's death, Hadley Mason flees into the Oregon wilderness to disappear. But when killers catch up with her, Hadley's life rests in the hands of Cooper Wilde, a wilderness-survival teacher who's determined to defend her.

KIDNAPPED AT CHRISTMAS • by Maggie K. Black
When journalist Samantha Colt is kidnapped and wakes up on her boss's porch, she can't remember how she got there. Somebody wants to harm her, and her boss's house sitter, soldier Joshua Rhodes, puts his life on the line to guard her.

DEADLY SETUP • by Annslee Urban
Set on clearing her brother's name, Paige Becker returns home...and finds herself a killer's next target. Now she must rely on her ex-boyfriend Seth Garrison—the detective who arrested and charged her brother with murder—to save her life.

LOOK FOR THESE AND OTHER LOVE INSPIRED BOOKS WHEREVER BOOKS ARE SOLD, INCLUDING MOST BOOKSTORES, SUPERMARKETS, DISCOUNT STORES AND DRUGSTORES.

LISCNM0916

*When a mysterious stranger washes up in her town with
no memory of his past, Deputy Sheriff Audrey Martin
must keep him safe from the men trying to kill him.*

Read on for an excerpt from
IDENTITY UNKNOWN,
the exciting conclusion to
NORTHERN BORDER PATROL.

Deputy Sheriff Audrey Martin sang along with the
Christmas carol playing on the patrol-car radio. The radio
crackled and buzzed before the sheriff's department
dispatcher, Ophelia Leighton, came on the line. "Unit
one, do you copy?"

Thumbing the answer button, Audrey replied, "Yes,
Dispatch, I copy."

"Uh, there's a reported sighting of a—"

The radio crackled and popped. In the background,
Audrey heard Ophelia talking, then the deep timbre of
the sheriff's voice. "Uh, sorry about that." Ophelia came
back on the line. "We're getting mixed reports, but
bottom line there's something washed up on the shore of
the Pine Street beach."

"Something?" Audrey shifted the car into Drive and
took off toward the north side of town. "What kind of
something?"

"Well, one report said a beached whale," Ophelia
came back with. "Another said dead shark. But a couple
people called in to say a drowned fisherman."

Her heart cramped with sorrow for the father she'd lost so many years ago to the sea.

She brought her vehicle to a halt in the cul-de-sac next to an early-model pickup truck where a small group of gawkers stood, and she climbed out.

"Audrey." Clem Previs rushed forward to grip her sleeve, his veined hand nearly blue from the cold. "Shouldn't you wait for the sheriff?"

Pressing her lips together, she covered Clem's hand with hers. "Clem, I can handle this," she assured him.

About ten yards down the beach, a man dressed from head to toe in black and wearing a mask that obscured his face struggled to drag something toward the water's edge.

Audrey narrowed her gaze. Her pulse raced. Amid a tangle of seaweed and debris, she could make out the dark outline of a large body. She shivered with dread. That certainly wasn't a fish, whale or shark. Definitely human. And from the size, she judged the body to be male.

And someone was intent on returning the man to the ocean.

Don't miss
IDENTITY UNKNOWN by Terri Reed,
available wherever
Love Inspired® Suspense books and ebooks are sold.

www.LoveInspired.com

LISEXP0916